*A Cornish Summer
at Pear Tree Farm*

A Cornish Summer
at Pear Tree Farm

Angela Britnell

Where heroes are like chocolate – irresistible!

Published 2022 by Choc Lit Limited
Penrose House, Crawley Drive, Camberley, Surrey GU15 2AB, UK
www.choc-lit.com

Printed and bound in Great Britain
by Clays Ltd, Elcograf S.p.A.

This book is for all of the "Cousin Jacks" who left their homes in Cornwall – 250,000 of them between 1861–1901 – because the decline of the mining industry left them struggling to survive. To provide for their families, they took their skills all around the world but never forgot where they came from, which is why you'll find pasty shops in Mexico and saffron cakes eaten in the Caribbean.

Acknowledgements

Amazingly this is my fifteenth book for Choc Lit, so I'd love to give special thanks to all of the loyal readers I've been fortunate enough to gather along the way for their unflagging support and enthusiasm for my trans-Atlantic romances.

Special thanks to the Tasting Panel readers who said "yes" and made publication possible: Elisabeth Hall, Lynda Adcock, Nicola Whittaker, Sarah Hartmann, Ruth Nägele, Joy Bleach, Janice Butler, Amy Nordon, Yvonne Greene, Donna Morgan, Fran Stevens, Lorna Baker, Sharon Walsh, Alma Hough and Gill Leivers.

Chapter One

'Why don't we buy some yurts? Everybody has them these days.' Lowena frowned at the calendar on the kitchen wall with its sparse number of red crosses marking the bookings for June.

'What's with the "we"?' Nessa stood up for herself, a rare enough occurrence to make her older sister's dark eyebrows shoot skywards. 'In case you've forgotten the campsite is my business.'

'Fine. I'll stand back and let you run Mum and Dad's pride and joy into the ground if that's the way you want it.'

She held her tongue. The only reason Ethel and Joe Vivian went into the tourist business thirty-five years ago was because Pear Tree Farm was losing money – they soon discovered that generally speaking campers were more profitable and easier to deal with than cows.

'Bookings pick up from mid-July onwards after all the kids get out of school and if this amazing weather holds I'll get more impulse visitors too.' Her sister continued to stare at the calendar. 'Remember I've got several permanent guests who bring in a steady income—'

'For heaven's sake be realistic, Nessa.' Her sister scoffed. 'We both know the Greens have paid the same pitiful rent for the last thirty years despite turning a corner of your land into their own little kingdom and you've let that idler Crispin stay for at least eighteen months now in return for doing a few odd jobs.'

Lowena didn't understand that Jack and Polly,

transplants from Birmingham who never went back after a week's holiday, were like family to her and their old bright pink VW Camper was part of the landscape. And Crispin? The proud ex-soldier turned up on the doorstep one rainy night and when she saw how much it cost him to ask if he could pitch his tent in her field in return for work Nessa couldn't send him away. Didn't everyone need a break sometimes? He did far more than odd jobs around the place and without him she'd struggle to cope.

'You're forgetting the orchard and my home-grown vegetables.'

'A few heads of lettuce and punnets of strawberries in the summer and the occasional basket of pears every October?'

'It's a lot more than that.' She lifted her chin. 'Anyway I'd already wondered about getting a couple of yurts for the top field but have you seen the price of them? They cost thousands of pounds.'

'Ask for a bank loan.'

'I'd prefer not to get into debt.' How she said that without her nose turning into a gargantuan version of Pinnochio's was nothing short of a miracle. Thank God her sister didn't know about the red bills and overdraft letters hidden in the junk drawer.

'That's sensible.' The tone implied "sensible" wasn't something her older sister expected from Nessa. 'If you cleared out the house you could offer bed and breakfast. People love to stay in characterful old farmhouses.' Lowena's scathing gaze swept around the cluttered kitchen. 'I've offered to help you sort through Mum and

Dad's stuff millions of times. How you can live in all this mess I honestly don't know.'

Some days she didn't either but huge pangs of guilt swamped her every time she considered getting rid of any of her parents' treasures. 'I'm used to it. It was this way when we were growing up. You know Mum was never much of a housekeeper. She preferred digging the garden to dusting.'

'But the house is yours now.'

Almost three years ago their parents died within six weeks of each other and her sister happily signed over her share of the farm to Nessa. Lowena's comfortable lifestyle included a beautiful house on a cliff top with expansive sea views over St. Mawes, about ten miles away.

'You're not Mum. It's time to make it your own.'

'I'll think about it okay and now if you're done criticising, I've got work to do.'

'And you think I don't?'

Lowena's busy life revolved around her husband, her teenage son and the myriads of volunteer organisations she was involved with. Nessa was granted a rationed one hour visit every Wednesday morning because that allowed her sister to go straight into Polgarth afterwards and organise lunch for the Sunset Club. She could only imagine what the local seniors thought of her sister's benign dictatorship.

'What's on the menu today?'

'Beef stew and dumplings followed by treacle tart with custard.' Lowena rolled her eyes. 'You'd think they'd appreciate something lighter when we're in the middle of a heatwave but when I suggested quiche and salad with ice cream and fresh fruit for pudding several of the committee members got very stroppy.'

'I expect they appreciate having a proper dinner put in front of them.'

'You're probably right.' A hint of satisfaction sneaked back into her sister's voice. 'I'll see you next week but if you need anything before then call me.'

For a second she could've sworn there was a shimmer of emotion in Lowena's bright blue eyes. Sometimes she sensed things weren't as perfect as they seemed under her efficient, capable surface. Nessa had never really taken to Antony, her brother-in-law. Although maths wasn't her own strong suit she didn't hold the fact he was an accountant against him but he *was* pompous and terminally dull; two characteristics she found hard to overlook. She adored her nephew but Kit had morphed into a typical surly seventeen-year-old who spoke in grunts and wanted little to do with his aunt any longer.

'I'll walk out with you.' She grabbed a plastic bucket of cleaning supplies. "Here Comes the Sun" needs cleaning before the new guests come on Saturday.'

'Why you picked such ridiculous names I'll never know.'

'Because they're fun and different and people like that.'

When their parents started out they bought six older model caravans of varying sizes which became Nessa's responsibility when she left school and joined them in the business. She'd lovingly repainted them in colours reminiscent of her favourite ice creams and maintained them to a standard that frequently surprised visitors. The names were a homage to her favourite summer songs and covered everything from The Beatles to ELO.

'Off you go and feed the elderly of Polgarth.' Nessa waved Lowena off and wandered across the farmyard, stopping for a moment to soak in the sight of her little domain basking in glorious sunshine. It wasn't an easy life but she wouldn't swap it for the world – although she would like to see more of that world one day.

Ward managed a thin smile when the estate agent handed over the keys. After two interminable months of back-and-forth paperwork, Tregereth House and the two acres of land it stood on was finally his.

'I'm thrilled for your sake it's been this fast.' Peter Endean looked very satisfied with himself.

He'd been horrified to discover the house buying process in England routinely took this long and couldn't help thinking it was a conspiracy between the solicitors and estate agents to snatch even more of his hard-earned money.

'I'm sure you'll be very happy once you're settled in your new home, Mr Spencer.'

The idea that a house could make him "happy" put a huge burden on a pile of bricks. If this move brought him any small measure of contentment, Ward would consider that enough of a miracle. 'Thank you.'

'Are you definitely going to explore taking in bed and breakfast guests once you've done the old place up?'

'Yeah, I think so or something along those lines anyway. I've been looking into what it takes and there are a lot of legal hoops to jump through first about changes to the property and my work status but I reckon I can pull it off.'

He'd travelled to Cornwall on a whim to see the area where Bill Tremayne, his six times great-grandfather, was born. The miner fled to America in the mid-1800s when the industry collapsed in Cornwall and ended up in what was known as the Copper Basin – a triangle of land covering parts of Tennessee, North Carolina and Georgia – never returning to his homeland. Something about the remoteness, the stunning rugged coastline and the slower pace of life had nibbled at the edges of Ward's tension until the wild idea of staying on crept in. He'd checked out a few properties online but when he was wandering around the centre of Truro one day his eyes were drawn to a photograph of Tregereth House in Peter Endean's window. The glossy picture couldn't hide the fact the large solid stone house with its old-fashioned sash windows and Cornish slate roof had seen better days but he'd immediately arranged a viewing. It might sound a bit New Age but after he discovered the word Tregereth meant mercy in Cornish that clinched it for him.

'Will you stay where you are until then? The house is habitable but it wouldn't be very comfortable.'

'I'd prefer to be closer. Do you have any suggestions?' His guesthouse was about ten miles away on the outskirts of Truro and his landlady considered it part of her job to stand in for Ward's mother while he was under her roof. 'I'd prefer somewhere I can come and go as I please.'

'Would a campsite interest you?'

'Perhaps.'

'It's not fancy there's a pretty little place right next

6

door.' He pointed to a stand of trees bordering the furthest field. 'The far west side of Pear Tree Farm adjoins your property over there. I know the young lady who runs it and could put in a word for you.'

'Are we talking about tents or what I call a travel trailer?'

'I believe Ms Vivian has both.' Endean pulled out his mobile. 'Would you like me to give her a ring?'

'Yeah.' He shaded his eyes from the bright sunshine while the man made a quick call.

'All set.' Endean beamed and shoved his phone away. 'If you drive along behind me I'll take you to meet her.'

He suppressed his urge to tell the man he could manage fine on his own. 'Thanks.'

'No trouble at all.'

Ward strolled over to his car and eased back into the little blue Kia. The vehicle was barely big enough to accommodate his six-foot-three frame but the pimply young man at the rental agency was spot on when he claimed it would be ideal for Cornwall's narrow roads and miniature parking spaces. The first time Wade met a bus and was forced to reverse back down a winding lane he'd given thanks for the car's miniature proportions.

A couple of minutes later they turned off the main road at a beautifully carved sign featuring lush rose-tinted pears so realistic Ward felt he could reach his hand out of the car and pluck one to eat. At the top of the short gravel drive was a charming stone farmhouse with dark pink roses trailing up and around the old oak door. Mud-splattered green wellington boots sat on the step ready for their next wearing and huge wooden tubs of colourful flowers stood sentinel either side of the entrance with similarly planted hanging baskets dotted along the front walls. Ward stepped out of the car and sniffed at the hint of fresh cut grass in the balmy air.

'This place sure is pretty.' His comment brought a satisfied smile to Endean's face.

'Ah, Ms Vivian this is Ward Spencer your prospective new guest and soon-to-be neighbour.'

Ward froze as a smiling, green-eyed, curvy brunette strode towards them. The woman's resemblance to Sophia hit him so keenly it almost brought him to his knees.

Chapter Two

Nessa wished Peter Endean would do or say something before the man wavering on his feet in front of her passed out. Despite his looming height and broad shoulders it struck her that he'd blow away in a good stiff Cornish breeze. His loose-fitting black linen shirt and baggy trousers did nothing to disguise his gaunt frame. Along with the unflattering square, black-framed glasses and close-cropped dark hair it combined to give her the impression of a troubled man.

'Are you all right? Why don't you come inside and sit down? I'll put the kettle on.'

'I'm fine and I don't need tea.' The deep, drawling American accent took her by surprise. 'You reminded me of someone for a moment. That's all.' He visibly pulled himself together. 'I won't take up any more of your time, Peter. I'll be fine with Ms Vivian if she doesn't mind showin' me around ... I'm sorry ma'am but I don't know your last name.'

'I don't mind at all and actually Vivian *is* my surname, it's an old Cornish one, but everyone calls me Nessa.'

'I'll leave you both to it then.' The estate agent nodded. 'Best of luck, Mr Spencer. It'll be a pleasure to see the old house brought back to life.'

She couldn't help being curious. There hadn't been a neighbour on that side of her land since she was a small child. One of her many impractical dreams had always been to buy the property and amalgamate it with hers, of course she'd never have the necessary money if she lived to be a hundred.

'If you come along with me, Mr Spencer, I'll show you around so you can decide if we'll suit you.'

'Call me Ward. Please.' A flicker of amusement softened his granite expression. 'In case you hadn't noticed I'm not a polite Brit.'

'Really? It's kind of you to point that out.' The wry comment made his lean face soften. Nessa launched into the usual spiel she gave new arrivals as they walked along and rattled off the history of the farm with its Vivian family connections going back to the seventeenth century. 'Were you thinking of a tent or caravan?'

'I haven't camped since I was a Boy Scout so I reckon a caravan will suit me better.'

'The caravans are fully equipped but there's also a laundry, toilet and shower block available for everyone to use. You might prefer it because the bathrooms in the caravans are—'

'Bijou?' His grey eyes brightened. 'That's Peter Endean's favourite way of describing rooms we'd use as a closet back home.'

'I must remember to use that word in future. It sounds much better than cramped.' She stopped outside a pale green caravan with gleaming silver trim. 'This is "Good Day Sunshine". She's the largest I've got available I'm afraid.'

'I don't need much.' He cocked his head. 'You're a Beatles fan?'

'Yes and older music in general really. My dad was a big fan of listening to classic rock stations on the radio and he amassed a large collection of vinyl records which I treasure. My caravans are named after our favourite summer songs.' Nessa blinked away a rush of tears.

'Tell me the others.'

'There's "Mr Blue Sky" …'

'ELO. Great choice. Sums up summer.'

Nessa wasn't sure why his approval pleased her so much. '"Lovely Day"—'

'Bill Withers. Yep, I'll give you that one.'

'"Summer Nights" …'

'John Travolta and Olivia Newton-John from Grease.' He raised one dark eyebrow. 'Everyone's musical tastes are different.'

'You're not a fan?'

'Uh not really my thing.'

'What about "Here Comes the Sun"?'

'Beatles again.' Warmth suffused his voice. 'Oh yeah. Love it.'

She gestured at the caravan. 'This is supposed to remind you of pistachio ice cream. I've painted them all to remind me of my favourite flavours because that's another obsession of mine. Fay Sampson at the village shop has a butterscotch ice cream to die for. If you have the chance to try it make sure she sticks in a chocolate flake and tops it with clotted cream.'

'That sounds awesome. I'm an ice cream lover too so we must be kindred spirits.'

A hot blush crept up her neck and she hoped he'd put her red cheeks down to the unusually warm weather.

At the top of the three steps she unlocked the door and Ward stepped in after her. Over the winter she replaced the dull brown upholstery on the built-in sofa and dining chairs with a pretty yellow and pale green chintz before adding soft dark green cushions large enough to tuck behind someone's back when they stretched out to relax. 'There's a double bedroom at the back and a single next to the bathroom. A lot of people on their own use that one for storage to spread out a bit. I know the kitchen is small but it's well-equipped.'

He gave everything a cursory glance. 'It'll do me.'

'Oh right.' His indifference peeved Nessa. 'If you don't mind coming back to the house, we can fill out the paperwork and sort out your deposit. How long do you expect to stay?'

'I'm not sure. I'm guessin' I need somewhere for at least a couple of weeks but I expect you're booked up.'

'It'll be fine. I wish we were full.' Her sister would reprimand her for being too honest. 'There are three long-term residents but apart from that there's only one family in at the moment. I do have a couple more families arriving on Saturday.' Nessa briefly mentioned the Greens and Crispin. 'If you need provisions there's a small convenience store in Polgarth. It's only a ten-minute walk from here or you can drive into Truro for the nearest supermarket.'

'The local place will do me.'

Usually her visitors were happy to chat but Ward Spencer didn't fit that mould or any other that she'd come across before. Maybe that was why he intrigued her so much. Her best option was to make a graceful retreat and leave him alone.

Ward flopped on the narrow sofa and rested his hands

behind his head. He couldn't help smiling when he stretched out and his feet touched the opposite wall. At first Nessa Vivian's uncanny resemblance to his ex-partner threw him for a loop but he soon realised that her frank affable manner was a million miles away from Sophia's calculated charm. He didn't need the stir of attraction she roused in him but what he *did* need was to stop lolling around, hop back into the car to go collect his things from the bed and breakfast then stop to pick up a few groceries. On the way over to the door the reflection in the small mirror fixed to the wall stopped him in his tracks. No wonder Nessa looked so worried earlier. Despite regaining some weight his cheeks were still hollow and the new brutal, short haircut he got before leaving Tennessee drew unwanted attention to his bony face. He was almost unrecognisable from his days as one of country music's hottest stars and that was fine with him. This venture – miles away literally and figuratively from the Nashville music scene – was his chance to leave the celebrity lifestyle behind him for good. Here no one would point him out in the street, cover their mouths with raised hands so they could whisper disdainful opinions on things they knew nothing about. Music was ingrained in his DNA but he needed to learn to live without it being the focus of everything he did – no matter how painful that was.

Ward flung open the door to get out of there.

'Welcome to Pear Tree Farm, Mr Spencer.' A little pixie of a woman, probably the same sort of age as his mother, stared up at him from the bottom of the steps with her frizzy purple halo of hair swaying in the breeze. 'Nessa popped in to let us know you've joined our happy band of campers. I'm Polly Green.'

He reluctantly made his way down to shake her outstretched hand.

'We host a barbecue every Thursday evening so we'd love you to come along tomorrow.' She chuckled. 'The sausages will be burnt to a cinder because my Jack thinks I prefer them that way, dear of him.'

It was a struggle to follow her curious accent but he caught the gist of her explanation. 'Why don't you tell the poor guy the truth?'

She broke into a peal of throaty laughter. 'You're not married, are you?'

'No.'

'I'm not surprised.' Her sharp blue eyes appraised him. 'Good looks only take a man so far and you won't be lacking in that direction once you eat a few pasties. We'll soon have you looking right as rain.'

The woman's bluntness stunned him into silence.

'Give and take. Compromise. Considering each other's feelings. That's what it's all about.' Polly wagged a finger in his face. 'Pale limp bangers don't even appeal to me any more and that's the God's honest truth.'

'Fair enough.' Ward geared himself to refuse the invitation but caught sight of Nessa heading their way. 'It sure is kind of you to include me. Can I bring anything?'

'Just yourself my love. If there's a full site it's different, everyone chips in then, but one more mouth to feed won't break the bank. We start about seven o'clock and our home's over there.' She pointed back to an old Volkswagen camper van painted an unmissable shade of bubble gum pink. 'You'll know we're ready when you smell the smoke.' Polly threw Nessa a satisfied smirk. 'You said he wouldn't come but you were wrong. He's into older women and I'm a prize cougar!' She gave a playful growl and sprinted off, her red sneaker clad feet barely touching the grass.

'I'm sorry.' Nessa looked mortified. 'Polly's a sweet lady but she doesn't have any—'

'Boundaries? Tact?'

'Don't worry I'll put her right and she won't bother you again. I thought you might appreciate a friendly welcome.'

He felt dreadful when her smile tightened. 'I'm sorry I didn't mean to be rude. Can we start over?' She gave a curt nod. 'I'm off to pick up my things but I'll be back later.'

'I'll let you get on.' Nessa's beguiling grin returned. 'In case you're interested Polly's favourite tipple is gin and Jack's a real ale fan.'

He'd add a stop at a liquor store to his list of errands. So much for Peter Endean's promise. Being left alone to do his own thing wouldn't happen here.

Chapter Three

'Are you coming over to Polly and Jack's tonight?' Nessa could guess Crispin's answer. She straightened up to ease the ache in her back. They'd spent most of the day clearing brambles in the upper field and working in a companionable silence that suited them both.

'Nah. You know me and people.'

'How can you resist Jack's gourmet charred bangers?'

'Easily.' Crispin picked up his axe again. Her sister couldn't be more wrong in calling him lazy. His stocky, muscular body seemed tireless. 'I'll finish off here if you want to get cleaned up.'

Nessa respected his privacy and knew when to back off. When they first met she assumed he was a lot older than her but after she fitted together the few nuggets of information he doled out she decided they were both in their mid-thirties. The main difference was that he hadn't stayed in the same safe corner of the world all of his life. Crispin's dark, hooded eyes reflected everything he'd seen and done. Things she probably wouldn't want to know about. She often thought his thick dark beard and shaggy, unkempt hair were a calculated form of protection. A warning to stop people getting too close.

'I don't want to take advantage of you.' She should stay to finish the job but a long soak in the bath sounded far more appealing.

'Your sister thinks I'm the one doing that.' He tilted the ghost of a smile her way.

'Lowena sees everything in black and white.' Nessa

needed him to know how much she appreciated having him around. 'I get far more back from you, Polly and Jack being here year-round than I give in return. You're a hard worker and I couldn't manage on my own.' Nessa loved hearing Crispin whistling the old Welsh hymns he loved as he went about his jobs and in the middle of winter it cheered her to see the lights glowing in her old friends' camper van.

A suspicious brightness glistened in his dark eyes before he turned away. 'This isn't getting the work done.'

'I'll leave you to it.' Nessa picked up the old cotton shirt she'd abandoned when the temperature soared and strolled back down the field. They were in the middle of one of Cornwall's rare stretches of hot, cloudless weather giving the impression it would continue forever. Everyone knew when it would break – in about another month on the day the kids got out of school – Sod's Law at its finest.

'It sure is a nice day.' Ward's thick silky drawl came out of nowhere and she spotted him lounging on the bench outside her front door. The late afternoon sun picked up a sprinkle of grey at his temples she hadn't noticed before.

Her bedraggled appearance was coming under amused scrutiny. This morning she only splashed cold water on her face, brushed her teeth and scraped her hair in a ragged ponytail. Her faded jeans and ancient grey T-shirt were now sweat stained and filthy. 'I've been up in the top field working and it's a sun trap. Did you want something only I'm about to have a desperately needed bath?'

'Yeah, I need a new light bulb for my shower.'

'I'll fetch one. Can you put it up yourself or shall I come and do it?'

'I'm sure I can manage.' His laconic drawl turned temptingly syrupy.

She made a quick escape before she said something that could be interpreted as flirting. The first winter after her parents died when she was at her lowest point she stupidly allowed a lifelong friendship with Jago Teague, whose farm was the other side of Polgarth, to deepen. A few months later his proposal came out of the blue – at least it did to her – and she had no hesitation in turning him down. Lowena was bewildered by her explanation that settling for anything less than the love she'd witnessed between her mum and dad every single day wouldn't have been fair on either of them.

'Their marriage wasn't perfect. No one's is. You and Jago could have a good life together. A family. Don't you want that?'

At the time she denied it although that was miles away from the truth. Most of the time she was simply too busy for introspection. Nessa stepped into the cool house and was thankful for the house's thick granite walls that kept it that way even on the hottest days. She swiped a bulb from her supply cupboard and made a mental note that she needed to stock up again before hurrying back outside. 'Here you are.'

'Thanks. I guess I'll see you later at the famous barbecue.' An unexpected sparkle brightened his pale eyes giving her a glimpse of a very different man. Nessa was out of practise but had the strong suspicion he was flirting with her. 'Enjoy your bath.'

Perhaps a cold, bracing shower was a wiser idea to knock some sense into her.

Ward blamed the fresh Cornish air for his uncharacteristic behaviour mixed in with the fact he was a regular, red-blooded male who'd been single too long. Too long in the sense of missing female company but not long enough to forget the fool he made of himself over Sophia. He'd been stirred by the energy surrounding Nessa when she came bounding down the gravel path with her sweat-soaked clothes stretched over wonderful, luscious curves. When she mentioned taking a bath it sent his brain, and other less cerebral parts of his body, zooming off into fantasy land. That's where it needed to stay.

For the last few days he'd been busy going back and forth to Tregereth and his to-do list had grown to mammoth proportions. It wasn't hard to see that a new roof was the first priority; the damp stains on several of the bedroom ceilings were a testament to that. Peter Endean had given him the name of a local builder he thought could help with that and all the other work to be done so contacting him was his next move.

A hint of smoke drifted in through the open door reminding him of the time. He didn't miss the unnatural chill of air conditioning that was crucial in the hot humid Tennessee summers. In this mild climate a cooling draft blowing through was all anyone needed. He'd overheard people complaining about the heatwave Cornwall was supposedly experiencing but it struck him as only a notch above pleasantly warm.

Ward grabbed the bottle of Cornish gin and six-pack of local beer off the table and stepped outside.

'Hello my love.'

Polly's raspy voice stopped him in the middle of locking the door. 'I was going to try my best to drag Crispin out of his tent to join us but Jack reckons I should leave him be.' Her massive gold hoop earrings jiggled as she shook her head. 'We don't often disagree.'

He hadn't met the ex-soldier face to face but once or twice caught a shadow of movement and glanced up in time to see a hunched shape disappearing out of sight towards an old khaki tent pitched in a far corner of the field.

'The two of you must be about the same age so I thought it would be nice if I could get you to meet. The poor soul could do with a mate.'

At a wild guess he'd say the last thing the elusive Crispin wanted was to have an unknown American foisted on him. The feeling was mutual.

Polly screwed up her face. 'You men are all the same. You'd still be in caves if women hadn't dragged you into civilisation.' She puffed out a sigh. 'I suppose I'll keep the peace and go along with Jack. Come on you can walk up with me.'

He'd only seen the pink camper van from a distance so wasn't prepared for the close-up version. 'Wow you've got a real homey set-up here.'

'That's because it *is* our home.'

If he tried to backtrack it would make the insult worse so Ward followed her along a short white gravel path and admired the neat garden. Colourful summer flowers scented the warm air and around the front door of the caravan a rambling pink rose climbed on a trellis. They walked on around and reached a well-tended vegetable patch.

'We've got home-grown tomatoes and onions with our sausages tonight and new potatoes,' she bragged. 'I'll send some home with you later.'

Ward couldn't imagine putting this much work into a place that didn't belong to him and found it interesting that Nessa would allow it. Maybe this was another example of the kindness he'd sensed when they met.

'Hello mate.' Jack waved a welcoming spatula. He wore a white chef's hat with the words "World's Best Cook" embroidered in bright scarlet. He'd set up the barbecue in a sheltered corner away from the caravan.

'I brought beer.'

'Good chap. Bring one over.'

'I'll be right there ... oh and that's for you Polly.' Her eyes lit up when he held out the bottle of gin.

'How'd you know that's my favourite tipple?'

'A little bird whispered in his ear.'

He caught the fresh tantalising scent of lemons and mint in the air as Nessa came to join them. She looked night and day different from earlier although Ward couldn't detect any make-up apart from a sheen of pink on her generous mouth. Her shiny, dark hair tumbled in a tousled mass of soft waves around her shoulders and she'd replaced her work clothes with a simple cotton dress. The faded purple and white flowery material showed its age but the cinched waist and low scooped neckline suited her hourglass figure. 'Our chef is desperate for a drink if you'll excuse me ladies.' Ward managed a brief smile then escaped but not before hearing Polly's chortled words.

'I think we've frightened him off.'

Ward held out two bottles to Jack. 'The guy in the store recommended this.'

'Can't go wrong with Tribute.' Jack opened them and passed one back. 'Cheers.'

They drank in companionable silence for a couple of minutes.

'Nessa's a good woman. Kind-hearted.' He continued to flip a pile of charred sausages. 'She's like a daughter to us.'

Ward guessed he'd been caught staring and took that as a veiled warning. One he'd be wise to remind himself of at regular intervals. 'I'm sure she is.' He took a welcome swig of the cool hoppy brew and let it slide down his parched throat.

'Come on let's join them.' Jack stabbed the sausages onto a plate.

The burnt offerings were placed in the middle of the white plastic picnic table and before Ward could stop her Polly dumped a heaping spoonful of tiny potatoes drenched in butter and chopped parsley on his plate along with another of fragrant grilled onions and a pile of miniature tomatoes. He swiftly stabbed a sausage before she had the chance to overload him with those too.

'So, where're you from Ward? By your accent I'm guessing somewhere in the south?' Polly knocked back a drink he suspected was more gin than tonic.

He stuck to the same bare-bones story he used with Peter Endean including a vague mention of a job in the

Nashville music business and the desire for a complete change. That was all anyone here needed. In Nashville his so-called friends had vaporised when scandal hit his career and he wasn't topping the charts any longer. He wanted these people to take him at face value and to earn their respect.

'What're you going to do with Tregereth House?'

'Live there.' The blunt response brought a touch of scepticism to Jack's gaze and Ward popped a tomato in his mouth. 'These sure are delicious. My grandmother used to grow a bunch every summer. Sweet as candy.' He tackled the sausage next and somehow managed to choke down the dry object. It wasn't difficult to let the others chatter between themselves without him having to contribute much more. Ward finished eating and made sure everyone else was done before he made his move to get out of there. 'It's been great to hang out with y'all but I ought to be goin'.'

'You can't leave yet. I've made a lemon tart for pudding,' Polly protested.

'I sure am sorry but I couldn't eat another bite.' That wasn't a lie. He'd got out of the habit of large meals when he was performing because it slowed him down onstage. The downward spiral of his troubles with Sophia and the loss of his music career hadn't helped and food still held little interest. That was another thing he hoped Cornwall might wave a magic wand over.

'I might make a move too,' Nessa said. The tempting smile she slid his way set Ward's pulse racing. 'Shall I take some food down to Crispin?'

'Yes lovey.' Polly heaped a massive pile of leftovers on

a clean plate. 'There. He'll make that do a couple of days I expect. Poor lad.'

If the man waded through the pile of "objects-that-used-to-be-sausages" covering half the plate he deserved a medal. 'I'll take him a couple of the beers if you don't want them all Jack?' Ward offered.

'Crispin doesn't drink.' Nessa's firm tone told him not to ask questions.

'Okay I'll leave them here then.' He stood up. 'Thanks for a great evening.'

'We'll see you next Thursday.'

Ward made a non-committal reply.

'It's all right I won't bite,' Nessa joked as they set off across the field together. 'I saw your long face when you came back from the grill and I'm guessing Jack put his big feet in it? They've got into the habit of watching out for me and especially since my parents died about three years ago.' A surge of defiance flared in her bright green eyes. 'In case you were wondering I don't need babying.' Her cheeks flushed.

'I'll remember that.'

'I'm going to run on with Crispin's food while it's warm.'

Ward watched her go and was pretty sure he'd been flirted with. Any sensible man in his position would steer well clear. If he kept reminding himself about Sophia that should help him to resist Nessa but he suspected the sooner he moved out of Pear Tree Farm the better.

Chapter Four

Her parents' overstuffed wardrobe stared back at Nessa as if daring her to spring open the doors.

'You're not Mum. It's time to make it your own.'

Lowena's words had stuck in her head and niggled away until she'd been forced to concede her sister had a point. The five bedrooms were crammed to overflowing and it was impossible to get into the attic and downstairs wasn't much better. It'd always been necessary to move a pile of clothes or magazines before sitting down and the dining room hadn't been used in forever because that was the last-ditch storage spot when everywhere else filled up.

She dragged armfuls of clothes on the bed and started to jam them into a black plastic bag. Her determination faltered when she came across the suit her mum wore to Lowena's wedding. Nessa stroked the soft purple silk before folding it and setting to one side. Her heart missed another beat when she unearthed her father's old brown-and cream- checked cardigan. She lifted it to her nose and savoured the earthy scent of his pipe lingering in the faded wool. Saving two things struck her as a reasonable compromise. Through a mist of tears she kept going and after a couple of hours this first and hardest room was finished. It took several trips to haul the mountain of bags downstairs but thankfully the bins would be emptied on Monday.

'Knock, knock. Anyone home?' Polly breezed in through the front door. 'Bloody hell what've you been up to?' Her friend gawped at the mound of black bags filling the hall.

'I've started on a clear-out.'

'Good for you. It's about time.'

'What do you mean?'

'I wondered how long it'd be before you'd sort your mum and dad's stuff. You know I loved them dearly but I never understood how they could let things get this bad.' Polly heaved a sigh. 'They were one as bad as the other and couldn't pass up a charity shop, a car boot sale or a flea market to save their lives. If it wasn't Ethel with her knickknacks it was your dad with his old records and local history books. I bet you've got all sorts of plans to spruce it up?'

'Not really. I mean … I've no clue.' Nessa stammered over her reply.

'There's no rush.' Her friend chuckled. 'You've a lot more to clear out before you get that far. Put the kettle on and you can tell me what put a rocket up you.'

For the last three years she'd kept things as they were but that wasn't working on so many different levels. After she'd tackled the house her next task was to make the business more profitable. She'd been content to let things drift far too long but all of a sudden that wasn't enough.

Ward stood outside the front door of Tregereth House and soaked in the incredible views around him. They were slap bang in the middle of the lush Polgarth Valley between Redruth and Truro and when the skies were as clear as today he could glimpse the shimmering sea in the distance. He hadn't expected to fall hopelessly in love with the land where his distant ancestor dug his living out of the ground but it cemented a place in his heart the first day he came here with Peter Endean.

Ever since his music career imploded he'd struggled to find a new focus to occupy him physically and mentally. He'd originally intended Tregereth to simply be his new home but the estate agent's suggestion of opening up the house to bed and breakfast guests really could be a realistic money-making project. If his plans brought in a few extra jobs and gave the area a small economic boost that might stop some of the local young people being forced to leave like Bill Tremayne all those years ago. He looked on it as payback. The only snag was he couldn't do it alone. His younger sister would make the ideal partner but if he approached Ashley the wrong way she'd suspect his motives. After he emerged from the mess with Sophia and could see beyond simply getting through the next day it forced him to pay more attention to his sister and her deteriorating marriage.

Before he had the chance to second-guess himself Ward strolled around to the sunny back garden and settled on one of the broken-down steps outside the kitchen door. A few minutes later his sister metaphorically tossed a bath tub full of ice water over his head.

'Me? Help you run a bed and breakfast in Cornwall? A glamping site? Are you mad? In case you've forgotten I've got a husband and a job here in Nashville. I know you don't think much of either but I can't help that.'

Jefferson Radnor had been a bone of contention between them ever since he sweet-talked Ward's teenage sister down the aisle a week before her nineteenth birthday. What grown man goes by the name "Bunny" anyway? His mother never appeared to see through his brother-in-law's slick façade but his father often seemed to be studying him as though trying to work out what lay behind Bunny's guileless blue eyes. Ashley used to be a sparkling, ambitious, intelligent young woman set to take on the world but after a decade of marriage to her controlling husband she'd been ground down to a shadow of her former self. There were always excuses why she didn't visit and on the rare occasions when she and Bunny did turn up at their parents' home she barely spoke. She never gave an opinion on anything until her husband had his say first at which point she'd agree with him. Ward got the sense she was frightened but when he cornered Ashley alone and begged her to tell him the truth – no matter how ugly – she brushed him off and told him to mind his own business.

'I really need your advice, Ash. I'll pay for your ticket.' Away from Tennessee he might be able to talk some sense into her. 'I need your vision. You've worked in hotels since you left school so you know what people are looking for. It's not my wheelhouse.'

'Then why come up with this crazy idea in the first place? You know what I think you ought to do and—'

'That's not an option.' He cut her off before she travelled down the road of restarting his music career. 'I need a completely different challenge.'

'Anyway you're exaggerating my non-existent talents.'

'Come on, Ash you're in charge of the cleaning team at one of the top hotels in Nashville and Dad told me they offered you a managerial role. Why did you turn that down anyway?'

'I had to. Bunny wouldn't have liked ...'

He didn't press when her voice trailed away. His brother-in-law was a successful insurance salesman but his ego wouldn't stand his wife having career goals of her own. 'Give me a couple of weeks. Help me get a concept together then I'll run with it from there.' Ward sensed her waver. 'You'd love it here. It's beautiful. Peaceful. The weather's awesome. Mild and sunny.' He chuckled. 'They're callin' it a heatwave but the high is only in the low eighties and there's no humidity. We get an occasional shower during the night or early in the morning so the gardens are still incredible.'

'They'll hire you for the Cornwall Tourist Board if you keep this up.'

'Is it workin'?'

'I can't. I'm real sorry.' Ashley's voice was suffused with regret.

After she hung up on him Ward knew if he wasted time going over what he'd said or didn't say right it would get him nowhere. He walked back around to unlock the front door and stepped into the generously proportioned square hall. According to the estate agent the house was built by one Henry Thomas in the late-eighteenth century when copper mining was at its peak and the area around Gwennap where Bill Tremayne worked was known as the richest square mile in the world. Thomas's shrewd investments made him one of the most successful adventurers, as they were known in the industry, but he wasn't a reckless man. He had no interest in an extravagant design to show off his new wealth which was why Tregereth resembled a typical Cornish farmhouse, albeit a sprawling eight-bedroomed one.

There was an air of neglect to the place because it hadn't been lived in for over twenty years. The last owner was an Australian who inherited it from a distant cousin but never visited and made the decision to sell the very week Ward started his property search. He wasn't a superstitious man but couldn't get away from the idea that that must be some sort of omen.

Ward headed up the curving mahogany staircase, his fingers brushing over the rub marks left behind by generations of people on their way to bed. He yanked his battered moleskin notebook from his pocket ready to scribble down any ideas. In the old days it would've been for song lyrics or fragments of tunes bugging his brain but that muse was long gone. The first door he tried creaked open when he gave it a slight shove and he surveyed the empty bedroom. Nothing could hide its elegant proportions and the incredible views over the gardens from its floor to ceiling windows. He wandered into the bathroom next door where the fixtures were old but functional since he'd had the electricity and water turned back on. He could always stick a few buckets around if the weather changed and rain came in before the roof was replaced. There were a few bits of furniture left around the house and although the kitchen needed a major update it was useable for now – he'd stay well away from the intimidating cast-iron range and stick to using the old electric oven. If he bought a bed and a few basic household items, there was nothing to stop him moving in immediately. It would put a wise distance between himself and Nessa.

A pang of regret struck when he pictured her teasing smile. If he could talk her into having dinner with him tomorrow that would give him the chance to break the news of his impending departure and, after a glass or two of wine, broach the subject of his plans for Tregereth. Ward didn't see his ideas being in direct competition with her business but had the uneasy suspicion she might not agree.

Chapter Five

'Evenings like this are hard to beat.' Nessa strolled along Primrose Lane beside Ward. The heat of the day had eased and the sun's soft glow dappled through the trees bathing everything in a pale golden light.

'Yep, it sure is pretty. Back home we'd be sweatin' still.' He gestured towards Polly and Jack striding out ahead of them. 'They're an energetic pair, aren't they?'

When he knocked on her door this afternoon she felt sure that a foursome for dinner wasn't what he had in mind but Polly was helping her sort out one of the spare bedrooms and shamelessly wangled an invitation out of him.

'They've got about twenty years on me but I struggle to keep up with them sometimes. When they moved here they were a similar age to my mum and dad so the four of them became best friends. They're like family to me.'

He glanced around as they reached the first straggle of cottages leading into the village. 'Let me guess the church is thirteenth century, the pub we're goin' to has been there almost as long and most of the houses are at least a couple hundred years old. There's one village shop with a nosy owner and perhaps a hairdresser and garage if you're lucky.'

'You've studied up on English villages.'

'My mom is a huge fan of y'all's TV programmes. She dragged my dad over here last year and came back drooling over all the cute places where people get murdered every five minutes.'

'Do you have a big family?'

'Not really.'

She sensed him retreat.

'Do you know where the name Polgarth comes from?' Ward changed the subject.

'Is the sky blue?' Nessa chuckled. 'My dad was a local history buff and told me stories about the village and this area instead of reading me fairy tales. The word Pol means a pool in Cornish and garth is a garden or enclosure. Polgarth and the valley in general were sparsely populated until the mid-nineteenth century when the old mining industries west of us failed. A lot of men moved overseas to continue mining but others turned to farming or found jobs in the china clay industry so were looking for homes closer to their work. The village hasn't changed much since I was a child.' She gave a rueful smile. 'I still know ninety-five per cent of the people who live within a five-mile radius. To most of them I'll always be Ethel and Joe Vivian's little girl.'

'Does that bother you? Isn't it hard to carve out your own identity?'

She thought a moment before answering. 'Most of the time I'm fine with it.'

'And the rest?'

Nessa couldn't open her heart to this man who was little more than a stranger. Even the chance to holiday somewhere she wasn't known was an intoxicating prospect. There was never any spare money for luxuries like that though.

'None of my business.' His smile edged back, blurring the edges of his sharp features. She got the impression he wasn't fighting so hard today to hold them in place and liked the difference it made to his appearance. 'I've gotta say I'm grateful for your failed mines because without them I wouldn't exist.'

'You?'

'Yeah, I've got a small amount of Cornish blood from my dad's side of the family. Bill Tremayne was my six times great-grandfather and he worked in the small Wheal Rosen mine near Redruth but left the area back in the mid-1800s and settled in Polk County, Tennessee. It was a big copper mining area.'

'That's where you're from?'

He shook his head. 'The later generations got away from mining and moved about seventy odd miles northeast to the Knoxville area. That's where I was born but we moved to Nashville when I was little because my father's country music career started to take off. He got to be a pretty well-known singer/songwriter with a string of hits and was invited to be a member of the Grand Ole Opry at a pretty young age – that's considered a big deal in Nashville. Latterly he got tired of performing and changed into managing other acts instead. He's semi-retired now and just takes care of a few of his older clients.'

At the barbecue he glossed over his own career, giving no details, and she guessed he'd clam up if she asked about it now. 'So, it wasn't exactly a coincidence you bought a house here?'

'Yes and no. I only came to see where Bill came from but I never expected to ... be drawn to the place this way.'

She sensed his embarrassment. 'Cornwall's easy to fall in love with.'

The conversation ended as they caught up with their dinner companions.

'Are you two comin'?' Jack held the pub door open.

Polly swooped in to grab for Nessa's arm and dragged her in past the men giving Nessa no chance to warn Ward about the low beams.

'Shit!'

The loud crack of head meeting solid oak made her wince.

'I guess Yanks can't read.' Benjy Martin sniggered from behind the bar. The landlord wasn't one of Nessa's favourite people but she had to admit there *was* a very obvious sign pinned to the first beam.

'Are you okay?' She hardly dared to catch Ward's eye. 'Why don't you sit down with Polly while I help Jack with the drinks?' He nodded and trailed off after Polly, still rubbing his head.

'Sorry we barged in on your date.' Jack gestured towards his wife as he and Nessie headed to the bar. 'Someone can be a bit oblivious sometimes.'

'It's okay. I wouldn't call it a date anyway.' Maybe later she'd discover if that's what he'd intended it to be. A little flutter stirred in the pit of her stomach. It'd been so long since she'd been interested in any man Nessa had almost forgotten the excitement of that initial zing. Was it vain to think he felt it too?

Ward put his clumsiness down to the distraction of Nessa's swaying hips when she walked in front of him, a tempting sight under her floaty yellow and white dress, dotted with sunflowers.

'This was a good idea,' Polly said. 'That poor girl rarely

gets a break. She works all the hours God sends to keep the place together.'

'Why isn't the site full when summer is in full swing and Cornwall is such a popular place?' A trickle of guilt sneaked through him because he wasn't being totally upfront with these questions. It was no good planning to open up Tregereth House to guests if no one was going to come.

'The problem is people want entertainment these days. Something for the kiddies to do. It's daft to my mind when there's a lovely beach only a few miles away and more beautiful walks than you could fit into a week's holiday but there it is.'

'She's right.' Nessa set down a pint of Tribute in front of him. 'My sister wants me to think of doing bed and breakfast but I'm not sure. Anyway forget that for now. Let's not put a damper on the evening.'

Despite her attempt to brush it off his heart sank anyway.

'What do y'all recommend?' He picked up a menu.

'I'm having my usual scampi and chips,' Jack said.

'What about you, Polly?' Ward asked.

'I fancy a pasty. I haven't had one in ages and I don't make them myself.'

'Are they difficult?' He'd eaten several of the stuffed meat pies popularised by the miners when he'd been out house hunting with Peter Endean and discovered he had no lack of appetite around them.

'Not really.' Nessa quirked a smile. 'But remember she's from up north and they don't know how to make a proper pasty.'

'Hers are wonderful.' Polly sighed. 'You'll have to get her to make you one. The pastry melts in your mouth.'

'Couldn't you sell them to the campers?'

'Do you know how many regulations there are about food hygiene these days?'

He struggled to come up with another suggestion. 'I'm guessin' you've got pear trees? Could you capitalise on them?'

'There are a few in the walled garden behind the house. I make pickles and jams that I give away to friends and family but selling them would be tricky and wouldn't make my fortune anyway.' Nessa's smile was forced. 'I don't know about you lot but I'm starving.'

Ward took the hint. 'Put me out of my misery and tell me what Toad in the Hole is? I sure hope that's not a literal description.'

Jack guffawed. 'Don't be daft, boy. It's a traditional English dish. You start by laying half-cooked sausages in a baking dish then pour batter around them and cook it in the oven.'

He found it a struggle to keep a straight face when Nessa's eyebrows shot up at the word sausages. 'I reckon I'll give the fish and chips a try. This is my treat tonight. Nessa, would you mind helpin' me order in case the clown behind the bar can't understand my accent?'

'Of course.'

They pushed their way through to the bar.

'Mr Spencer?' A ruddy faced older man appeared at Ward's side. 'I'm George Yeatman. The builder. You left a message for me about—'

'Oh yeah.' Ward felt his cheeks heat. 'Someone said you

might be the man to contact about doing a few repairs to Tregereth House.'

'Sounded a fair bit more than repairs to me, mate.' Yeatman's deep belly laugh turned into a nasty cough that took him a moment to control. 'Getting her on your side?' He nodded at Nessa with a knowing wink. 'Good idea. You don't want to be bad neighbours.'

'Why would we be?' Her taut expression didn't alter when he muttered about getting a new roof.

'Mr Yeatman, if it's convenient could you pop up to the house tomorrow and we'll have a good chat then?'

'Call me George, boy. Can't come on a Sunday. I'm afraid the wife would string me up. Our boy and his family always come over from St. Agnes for a roast. I'll be there first thing Monday morning.' He touched his cap and sidled off.

'You ready to order?' Benjy Martin unintentionally came to the rescue and Ward let Nessa take over. As soon as he paid she buttonholed him again.

'Is there a chance now I'll find out the truth behind why a single man – at least that's my assumption – bought a huge old house in Cornwall?' She gave him an arch look. 'I may not like the answers but I prefer that to being in the dark.'

Ward scooped up the four sets of cutlery wrapped in paper napkins. 'You're right about the single part but could we talk after dinner about the rest? On our own?'

'You don't want our dinner companions to hear?'

'It's kind of private.' He'd prefer to suffer the full extent of Nessa's anger on their own instead of in front of an audience.

'Fine.'

Ward couldn't claim that the rest of the evening was awkward because the two women kept up an endless stream of conversation despite seeing each other every day. Jack should've been a diplomat because he discussed the unpredictable Cornish weather and his plans to extend their vegetable patch over the winter, clearly realising something was up between him and Nessa.

They were a quieter group walking back to the farm and Jack deflected Polly's suggestion of ending the evening with coffee at their caravan.

'I'm tired, love. Let's call it a night.'

Ward caught Nessa's puff of relief when they were left alone.

'Would you like to see the pear trees?'

That slight hint of unbending encouraged him. 'I sure would.'

They made their way along the gravel path and once their hands accidentally brushed sending a jolt of awareness through his blood.

'Pear trees are tricky to grow in Cornwall because of the damp climate but they were Mum's favourite fruit so my dear father built a protected garden for her to have a go.' She stopped in front of a wrought iron gate set into an old brick wall. 'They need either the reflected heat of a south facing wall or something like a greenhouse or polytunnel. You have to watch out for insects especially pear midge.' Nessa opened the gate and waved him on through. 'The famous Pear Tree Farm orchard.'

The self-deprecating remark couldn't erase the pride in her voice and he saw why when they stepped inside.

Either side of the narrow path they strolled along were narrow beds crammed with a huge variety of colourful flowers and it brought to mind the small vase of delicate sweet peas gracing his kitchen table when he moved in. Dominating the rest of the garden were two vegetable beds.

'Wow, I didn't expect all this.' His comment made Nessa blush. 'I'm not very up on gardening but are those potatoes and carrots?' Ward pointed to the plants closest to them.

'Yes you know your veg.' She laughed. 'Then I've also got courgettes, cucumbers, tomatoes, broad beans and rhubarb. Plus some soft fruits – strawberries, raspberries and blackberries. My strawberries are doing really well this year. This weather suits them. Crispin picked a whole lot today.'

'Must take up a lot of your time keepin' it all watered?'

'Not yet. The occasional showers we're getting are keeping it going for now but if we don't get anything substantial soon things could get tricky.' She gestured to several tall bamboo stands. 'I'm sure even you can guess what those are?'

'Green beans.'

'Yep only we call them runner beans. I'll plant some winter veg later like cabbage, cauliflower and kale.'

'Have you always been keen on gardening?'

She looked thoughtful. 'It was my mum's thing and she taught me everything she knew. She preferred digging in the dirt to cleaning the house or cooking and I'm the same.' Nessa chuckled. 'My sister is the complete opposite. Lowena wages a continual war on the dust in her immaculate house and is a gourmet cook. She despairs of me.'

'I reckon it's a good thing we aren't all the same.' Ward glanced around. 'What's the greenhouse for?'

'So I can start off plants early in the year before putting them out. It gives them a head start before they go in the ground.' She ran her fingers through her hair and sighed. 'I've got another field up behind this and one day I'll have the time to turn the ground over and grow a wider variety of vegetables there.'

'You'll do it.' Ward recognised the broad streak of persistence buried under her soft exterior. 'So where are the famous pear trees?'

'Up here.'

He followed her and smiled when she reached out to stroke the vibrant green leaves on the first tree they came to. 'They're taller than I expected. Shows what I know about fruit trees!'

'They can grow up to about six metres and you've got to plant them roughly the same distance apart. These four of the Williams variety have survived. I think you call them Bartlett in America – and the two at the far end of the row are Conference pears.'

'They were clearly important to your mom and we all need something that matters to us.'

'What's yours or is that another secret?' Nessa's husky whisper shot straight to his core.

He recklessly took a step closer and her own light intoxicating fragrance surrounded him capturing the scent of long summer days and even longer summer nights. 'It used to be music.'

'Used to be?'

'Yeah. I was in the business a long time but I got out of it a couple of years ago.' Ward jerked away and pretended to examine the tree. 'Looks like your fruit is comin' on well.' He'd broken the spell with good reason. For a few foolish seconds he almost forgot that Nessa needed answers not seduction. 'How about we sit down?' A wood bench, bleached with age, nestled in one corner and a rainbow cloud of pink and cream roses climbed the nearest wall sending their intoxicating scents to saturate the warm air.

'It's so bad I don't need to be standing to hear what you've got to say?'

'I don't reckon so but ... you might.'

'Mum used to escape here when she needed to think and work things out.' Nessa smoothed down her dress and settled on the bench. 'Try it.'

By the time he stumbled over explaining his plans for Tregereth the atmosphere had turned to ice.

'So, you're going to open a fancy bed and breakfast and glamping site right next to my struggling business.' Her flat tone bothered him more than if she'd exploded with justifiable anger. 'I might as well stop wasting my time and clearing out the house hadn't I?'

'Mine will only have half a dozen rooms at most and a couple of yurts. Surely there's enough business for both of us?'

Nessa's head dropped. 'You haven't heard anything I've said. Oh, just go away and leave me alone.'

Ward refused to beg for sympathy so he silently did as she asked. He'd save telling her about his tentative idea to move out sooner than anticipated when he'd firmed up his plans.

Back at the caravan he opened the wardrobe and pulled out the guitar stashed away behind his clothes. Smoothing his hand over the cherry wood surface his thumb caught on the remnants of the distinctive logo for Spence + Sophia. He should've left the guitar behind in Nashville along with everything it represented.

Ward shoved the precious instrument back in the case and practically threw it in the wardrobe. He sunk down on the bed and clutched his head in his hands. Why was nothing straightforward these days? Perhaps he should forget the whole ridiculous idea and get on the next airplane back to Nashville.

Chapter Six

Nessa pushed a lock of sweaty hair out of her face and sighed at the sight of her sister standing by her car and frowning at her watch. Lowena's dark blue linen dress and neat matching sandals were a dismal contrast to her own work-stained shorts and baggy T-shirt. She had hoped to be through in time to tidy herself up but miscalculated. Ten o'clock on Wednesday morning meant precisely that to her punctual sister.

'I was beginning to wonder where you were.'

'I've been hoeing the vegetables. If I don't keep on top of the weeds they run rampant this time of year. Come on in and I'll put the kettle on.'

'Aren't you going to change?'

She stretched out a thin smile. 'I'll wash my hands. That will have to do.'

In the kitchen, Nessa steered the conversation around to her nephew because her sister loved to brag about her only child's achievements.

'Kit's last report card wasn't up to standard. If he doesn't work harder he'll never get into a decent university.' The furrows in her forehead deepened. 'He's dropped out of several school clubs too and they're vitally important to show he's well-rounded. Kit says he's tired of them and we can't make him go.'

'What does Antony say?'

Lowena snorted. 'He's oblivious. Always in his own little world. He'll be furious if Kit doesn't make something of himself but he doesn't lift a finger to help.'

She studied her sister properly. The immaculate make-up did nothing to disguise the dark shadows or hide her unsmiling eyes. 'You're tired. Exhausted. You do too much.'

'If I don't …'

'What's going to happen? Will the world come to an end if you don't cook a full Sunday roast every week? And all of the groups you volunteer with – can't someone else run them for a change? As long as Kit grows into a kind, decent human being isn't that what's important?'

'You don't understand.'

'Then make me. Help me out here.'

'Those things are all I have.' Lowena's pinched expression spoke volumes. 'Antony breezes in every evening after a so-called brutal day at work and flops in the chair holding out his hand for the gin and tonic I make for him. Kit treats the house like a hotel and me as a cook, laundry maid and chauffeur. And I don't need you telling me I've made a rod for my own back either.'

'Could you explain how you feel and suggest that things need to change?'

'You're so naïve.' Lowena scoffed. 'It's what comes of being single with no one else to consider. Marriage and having a family don't work that way.'

Nessa bit her tongue, forcing herself to calm down for a minute. 'I hoped I could help *you* for a change instead of it always being the other way around.'

'There's something more.' Her sister continued reducing a paper tissue to shreds pleating it over and over again. 'I think Antony's having an affair.'

'Antony? Surely not. Do you have any proof?'

45

'Nothing definite but he receives a lot of late evening phone calls and hurries off to another room or outside to speak.'

'Have you asked him who they're from?'

'Of course. He *claims* there's a problem at work but seriously? He's an accountant for the National Trust. For God's sake, Nessa, no one's going to ring him at eleven o'clock at night because the Lanhydrock café books aren't balanced.' A flush crept across Lowena's cheeks. 'I even checked his phone the other day but he's deleted his call history.'

She floundered around for a feasible explanation. 'Maybe he's planning a surprise party for your wedding anniversary next month?'

'Don't be ridiculous. I doubt he even recognises it's coming up and it's only our eighteenth so nothing special.'

Nessa wracked her brains for a way to help. 'Does Kit have much on this weekend?'

'I don't think so. Why?'

'Bring him here.' She caught her sister's surprise. 'You can whisk Antony off somewhere, just the two of you. If you're on your own with no distractions it might be easier to sort things out.'

'But you've got this place to run.' Lowena sounded dubious. 'Remember Kit's not the sweet little boy who loved to trot around the campsite after Aunt Nessa any longer.'

'He can help me out. I'm planning to start painting the bedrooms so I'll stick a brush in his hand.'

'You're mad but on your own head be it. I'll ask them.'

Her face hardened. 'If Antony says no I might just take off somewhere on my own.'

'Good for you.' Nessa glanced at the clock. 'You'll be late for the Sunset Club if you don't hurry up.' At the door her sister uncharacteristically pulled her into a tight hug.

'I'll give you a ring and let you know about the weekend. Why don't *you* tell *me* what's bothering you now?'

She didn't ask how Lowena knew something was up. On the surface they had little in common but their bond ran deep. This wasn't the moment to bring up Ward's plans to put her out of business. Of course he would deny it but the stark truth was that the slim number of visitors who came her way would evaporate once he opened his fancy site next door.

'I'm fine.'

'I expect to hear about it next week.'

Nessa clung onto a tight smile until Lowena had jumped into her car and driven off.

Ward perched on the steps outside the kitchen door enjoying the sunshine. He sipped his coffee and idly stared at George Yeatman's rough sketch again. He'd made the right choice in steering clear of fancy designers and hooking up with the plain-spoken man. The local builder had no problem telling him outright what would work, and what wouldn't.

'If we get a move on and we're lucky you might get your permission by September. It normally takes a good six to eight weeks after submitting the application. You'll have to deal with all the business regulations but I still reckon we should be able to get you up and running by Easter. Before we start anything you'll need a new roof.'

They'd shaken on it and George promised to come up with more detailed plans soon. There'd been no routine maintenance done for decades so there were rotten window frames to repair and the wiring and plumbing both needed to be upgraded. Along with that they'd reconfigure the bedrooms to accommodate the necessary en-suite bathrooms. The house was full of ugly, old carpets so they'd be ripped out and the oak floorboards sanded back to their original state. The kitchen was a project all of its own that he couldn't even think about yet. Completely redecorating throughout would be the final touch and a long way off.

Ward startled when his mobile jangled to life. 'Hi Ash. How're things back in Tennessee?'

'I need to know if you meant what you said.'

'In what way, kiddo?'

'Last week you asked for my help with this place you've bought.'

'Yeah of course I meant it.' He didn't point out the fact she'd turned him down.

'Good. I've gotta get away from here before I … can't.' There was a hitch in her voice. 'There are two conditions. If Bunny calls you haven't heard from me and you can't tell anyone there in Cornwall that I'm your sister. It's too risky. You'll have to make somethin' up … and don't ask because I'm not talkin' about it.'

'Okay. What about Mom and Dad? Do they know what's goin' on?'

'No. I'm sorry but you'll have to lie to them too. If you can't do that I'll find somewhere else to go.'

When he was ten years old his father took him to the hospital to see his new-born sister and placed the crying, red-faced scrap of a baby in his arms.

'Big brothers have one job, son and that's to look out for their siblings. Okay?'

He hadn't argued then and wouldn't now. 'Of course. When're you comin'?'

'I fly into London Friday morning. Can you pick me up from Heathrow?'

'Yeah, no problem. Email me your flight details.'

'You're the best and I mean that.'

'Yeah well you might change your mind when you see how much work there is to do here.' He tried to make light of the situation. After they finished talking he weighed his options and decided to get the afternoon train up to London tomorrow and stay the night near the airport. It was unlikely anyone here would guess their relationship because they were chalk and cheese as far as looks were concerned. Ashley took after their petite, blonde mother and Ward was the spitting image of his tall, lanky father.

For days he'd debated whether to go online and start his visa application. From the research he'd done, an Innovator visa, issued to people who wanted to set up or run a business in the UK, was his best bet. He had enough investment funds to back it up and fulfilled all the other criteria. With luck it could be approved in as little as three weeks, enabling him to stay for a maximum of three years. By then he'd either have made a success of the business or not. Ward hurried inside and settled at his laptop. Half an hour later he pressed the send button and leaned back in the chair, exhaling a satisfied sigh.

While his mood was on an upward trajectory, he headed out shopping. With Ashley on the way soon to join him it didn't make sense to delay moving into Tregereth a moment longer. He quickly tracked down what he needed in Truro and he managed to squeeze into his car an air mattress and pump, towels, bedding, basic kitchen and cleaning supplies and a couple of folding chairs. It left just enough room for his gear from the caravan. Ward's enthusiasm wavered as he drove into Pear Tree Farm past Nessa's house and parked next to "Good Day Sunshine". The second he stepped out of the car, Polly appeared out of nowhere.

'I've got a bone to pick with you. I've been talking to Dorrie Biscombe and her sister's boy works for George Yeatman. Told me some tale she did about you. Does poor Nessa know what you're up to?'

He should've asked the builder to keep his mouth shut but it was too late now.

'They reckon you're going to turn Tregereth into a posh bed and breakfast and use the land for "glamping". I'd never heard of such a thing but Dorrie says it's some sort of fancy campsite where people sleep in huge tent things.'

'Yeah she's right and they're called yurts.' Ward couldn't quite meet her inquisitive gaze. 'Nessa knows.'

'I bet she's not flaming happy about it.'

Understatement of the year.

'Thought not.' Polly cackled. 'That girl's made of tough stuff. She'll give you a run for your money.'

It'd be a waste of breath to explain. All he could do

was plough ahead and let the project speak for itself. 'I'd better get on and pack but I'm sure I'll see you and Jack around.'

'Not if we can help it.' Tossing her head made this week's towering coils of bright blue curls shake.

He left her to her indignation and retreated inside to collect his things. Luckily he hadn't brought much in the first place. He couldn't put off facing Nessa any longer and down at the house she flung open the door before he had a chance to knock.

'Good afternoon. Beautiful day isn't it?'

'Yeah.' Ward cleared his throat. 'I'm leavin' so I came to settle up. I'm sorry to leave you in the lurch but I'll pay you for the full time I promised to be here.' He'd pay her for a month if he could make things right between them.

'Leaving?'

He couldn't be sure if her voice was laced with relief or dismay. 'I need to be on site to work on the house.'

'Of course. Come in.'

Ward followed her into the kitchen and a blanket of silence hung around them as Nessa ran his credit card through and printed off a receipt.

'There you are. I've charged you for two weeks. We're square now.'

'No, we're not and I'm not talkin' about money. I owe you an apology. Let me get one thing right with you.' His heart thundered in his chest.

She'd done a good job of holding her emotions in check until his drawl thickened and turned husky. Memories flooded back of being with him in the walled garden. The tease of his cologne had mixed with the heady scent of her roses while the soft evening light picked up the threads of silver in his spiky dark hair. She'd been convinced he was on the verge of kissing her when he ruined everything.

'I don't suppose you'll believe me but I only bought Tregereth as a place to put down new roots.' He cleared his throat. 'I've had a challenging couple of years and need a change of pace. I'd love nothin' better than to tell you everything but—'

'We barely know each other.'

'Yeah.' The tips of his ears turned pink. 'Maybe we could put the business stuff to one side and—'

'I'm sorry but that's impossible.' She needed to be straight with him. 'Like it or not this place is part of who I am. If I was nicer I'd wish you luck with your venture but that's going a step too far.'

'You seem like a really nice person to me.'

She snorted. 'You're digging a deeper hole. When people use the word "nice" they usually mean a pushover.'

'No one in their right mind would ever claim that about you.'

The flash of insight scared her.

'Polly had a go at me. She reckons rumours are goin' around the village about what I'm hopin' to do with Tregereth. That's not the way I wanted things to go.'

'That's Polgarth for you.'

'I'd enjoy showing you the plans if you fancy coming over. They might not be as awful as you imagine and we might come up with some ideas for our mutual benefit.'

'Thanks for the offer, but let's leave it there.'

'Really?' Ward's voice dropped to a raspy whisper. 'You can do that? I'm not sure I can.'

'Well I'm sorry but you'll have to.'

'If that's the way you want it.'

Sadness threaded through his voice and for a second her resolution wobbled. Nessa reined it back in and at the door they exchanged stilted goodbyes. As soon as he walked away she retreated back into the house. It wasn't Nessa's habit to dwell on what might've been and she refused to start now.

Chapter Seven

'Okay big brother, do I get the guided tour now?'

Ward noticed his sister had changed into a loose floral summer dress but dragged back on the same long, grey cardigan she'd travelled in. In the last six months she'd gone from slim to scarily fragile. At the airport this morning he attempted to give her a welcoming hug but she winced so he hadn't touched her again. For some reason she'd dyed her blonde hair an unflattering bright red, washing all the colour from her skin.

'Sure. I thought we might go to the village pub for dinner in an hour or so to save us cooking?' Or I've got plenty of food here we can fix. You choose.' She looked wary as though he was trying to catch her out.

'I'm pretty tired I'd rather stay here.' A flare of panic darkened her expression. 'That's if you don't mind …? We don't have to—'

'Ash, I asked you didn't I?' Clearly Bunny hadn't been interested in her opinions on anything.

'Yeah but—'

'But nothing. It wasn't a trick question. We'll eat here.' Ward opened the front door. 'Let's get some fresh air first.' He grinned. 'Come and see my estate.' There'd been no one to show it off to before.

They chatted as they wandered around about how to bring the overgrown formal gardens back to life and reached the field to the west of the house that he'd earmarked for the glamping project.

'It should be ideal because it's basically flat and the

slight slope will help with drainage. I'm thinking of buying two good-sized yurts to start with, plus compost toilets and a solar powered bathroom yurt. All low-impact as far as damage to the land is concerned.'

'I haven't seen you be this enthusiastic about anything since …' The flicker of good humour faded. It didn't take a genius to guess she was thinking about the heady days when his star in the country music world was in its ascent and he seemed invincible. 'It's awesome. C'mon I want to see the rest of the house.'

They started in the bare entrance hall and Ward rattled off the potted history of the old building. 'Upstairs first?'

'Sure.' Ashley smoothed her hand over the bannister rail. 'You need to keep all these original features. People will appreciate them. We'll need to trawl the estate sales and flea markets for furniture and decorative pieces to suit this place. Modern stuff and reproductions would be a travesty.'

'See I knew I needed you here.'

They peeked in the first couple of empty bedrooms before he opened the next door to a much smaller one. 'This isn't big enough for guests so I reckon we can use it ourselves or keep it for storage. It still gives us five. They'll all need en-suites added of course, and my builder reckons we could convert the attic that runs the length of the house into more rooms if we want to expand one day.'

Ashley drifted past him like someone in a dream and stopped in front of an old wooden baby cot, its white paint chipped and faded. 'This was the nursery.' Her haunted expression sliced through him. 'If I needed a reminder about why I had to leave Nashville this does the trick … not that it's necessary.'

'What do you mean, Ash? I—'

'Don't. Not now.' She swiped at her eyes with the sleeve of her cardigan. 'When I'm not all over the place with jet lag and whatever, we might talk then but now I want to see the rest of your crazy new home.'

He'd go along with her for the moment. 'You asked for it. I've had no one else to bore with all this.'

'Bore away.'

It surprised him when she linked her arm through his. Maybe they could both find mercy here.

Lowena tossed a pile of red bank statements on the table. 'Before you get mad I wasn't poking around your things. I needed a pair of scissors to cut a thread off my skirt. Next time you try to hide something choose a better spot than your junk drawer.' There was a glimmer of sympathy in her deep blue eyes. 'Why didn't you tell me things were this bad?'

'You've got enough on your plate. Forget that for a moment and tell me what the story is with Antony? Couldn't you talk him into going away for the weekend?' An hour ago her sister and nephew turned up and Lowena brusquely announced she would be staying too. Kit had slouched off upstairs to dump his weekend bag and they hadn't seen him since although Nessa heard the back door slam and guessed he'd gone outside. Probably to escape being talked at or questioned.

'He's got a big meeting next week to prepare for. At least that's what he said.' Her sister snorted. 'I can't tell you anything more. I still want to know what you were uptight about last week.' Lowena picked up one of the statements. 'Was it because of this or something else?'

There was no point trying to hide the news. Nessa made a determined effort to sound unconcerned and explained about Ward's plans for Tregereth House.

'You brushed off a single, rich American who was interested in you?'

Trust her sister to home in on that snippet of information and ignore the rest. Normally Lowena concentrated her matchmaking skills on whether men were decent and trustworthy but presumably with Nessa still being unattached those qualities were going by the wayside.

'I have my pride.'

'A lot of good that will do you. Oh well we need to make a plan.' The brisk committee chair voice came out. 'I must say you're doing a good job of getting the house in shape but four rooms doing run-of-the-mill bed and breakfast won't make enough money to keep the bank manager happy. You need a more unique angle.' Lowena's frown eased into a satisfied smile. 'How about instead of farm-to-table, you offer garden-to-table classes? Offer people the chance to stay in a centuries old Cornish farmhouse while they learn the tricks of organic gardening from an expert.'

'Expert?'

'Don't put yourself down.'

Most days her sister made light of the time and effort she put into her vegetable garden so she'd no idea why all of a sudden it was considered a marketable skill.

'Polly's done a lot of seasonal work in cafes and restaurants hasn't she?'

'Yes. She's a great cook so can always pick up as much or as little work as she wants. At the moment she's taking a break.'

'That's perfect because quite honestly you're not a star in the kitchen so talk her into helping you out. You need to get her to focus on vegetarian and vegan recipes and you'll have a hit on your hands. People are into that whole lifestyle these days. If it takes off you could do a spot on the local radio or write a book.'

She almost asked what illegal substance was in her sister's tea. 'Assuming that Polly says yes I wouldn't know where to start with the classes.'

'If you don't know any teachers, I do. We can find someone to give you advice.'

Nessa was starting to feel steamrollered. 'Jack was an English teacher before they moved down here so he generally picks up work as a substitute and does private tutoring. I suppose he would help.'

'This is brilliant.'

'But it'll cost money to get off the ground. Money I don't have and can't get.'

'I've got money.' Lowena gave a triumphant laugh. 'Antony leaves the household budget to me and I'm always careful with it. I've done a little dabbling in the stock market over the last decade with the excess and I have to say I've done fairly well.' Two pink circles bloomed on her cheeks. 'I'm happy to invest half of it in you. I must hold onto the rest in case my marriage falls apart.' Her smile flickered back to life. 'Don't worry. I've no interest in getting involved in the day-to-day running. We both know that wouldn't work.'

'What about all the regulations about food preparation and so on?'

'I'll help you with that. I've learned all about it through my volunteer organisations and have several contacts at the local council.' Lowena stuck out her hand. 'Do we have a deal?'

Before Nessa knew what happened they were shaking hands.

Ward hadn't appreciated how hard it would be to lie to their parents. 'I'm sorry Mom but I haven't heard from Ashley in weeks.'

'Poor Bunny's been on the phone every five minutes. He's worried sick about her. She said she was taking a few days off work to visit an old friend in San Francisco which is totally out of character but when he called to check she'd arrived safely, Ruby hadn't heard from her.' His mother sighed down the phone. 'He got madder than a wet hen when I suggested he contacted the police. Bunny said he wasn't having their private business trawled through by any nasty detective. What do you think he meant?'

He muttered something non-committal.

'Your father's been sayin' for ages they've got marital problems but I think he's imagining things. I know Ashley isn't ... cheerful like she used to be and she's gone dreadfully thin but between you and me I think they're struggling to start a family.' She puffed out a sigh. 'Hang on a sec your daddy's buggin' me. He wants to talk to you.'

'Really? Uh okay.' That set off alarm bells. His father was usually content to get the news second hand.

'Hi son. Your mother's fretting and I don't like that.'

'No sir.'

'You and Ashley have always been thick as thieves and I'm bettin' my bottom dollar she'll contact you if she hasn't already. I'm not askin' you to break any promises you've made to her but I need to know she's all right.' His gruff voice cracked.

Ward wrestled with his conscience. 'She's okay Dad but—'

'Don't say any more. Bunny won't hear anythin' from us if I have to zip your mom's mouth shut. You take good care of my girl. We've let her down.'

The conversation left him more conflicted than ever. He was mulling over whether to tell his sister that their father dragged the truth out of him when Ashley strolled into the kitchen. The baggy grey cardigan was swinging loose and everything about her seemed less uptight already. Decision made.

'My builder will be here in a few minutes.' A flicker of dismay crossed her face. 'He's in the middle of drawing up the planning application and needs my input. Stick to the story we've agreed about why you're here and it'll be fine. I really need you in on this.'

'What if he gets the wrong impression and thinks I'm your …' She wrinkled her nose. 'Oh Lord it's so weird I can't even say it.'

'If it keeps you safe and under Bunny's radar then Yeatman and everyone else can think what they like.' A tiny nub of regret settled in his gut. Any slim chance that remained with Nessa would disappear like snow in the sun when the gossip reached her. A loud knock on the kitchen door ended that depressing train of thought. 'Hi George.' He introduced Ashley and spun the old-friend-of-my-sister story.

'Pleased to meet you.' Yeatman tipped a finger to his ancient cloth cap. 'What do you think of Cornwall so far? Too bloody hot for me but maybe you're used to it?'

Before she had a chance to answer, Ward steered the man's attention away. 'You reckon six to eight weeks for the planning application? That should give us time to get some outside work done before the weather changes.'

'Plenty. If it's all right with you we could go ahead with the roof next week. My mate and his crew have a few days spare between jobs and they're the best you'll get. After they're done I'll make a start on the window repairs.'

'Sounds good.'

Yeatman scratched his head. 'I've heard a few rumblings in the village. Folk griping about outsiders coming in to change things.'

'But Tregereth has stood empty for over twenty years. If things go as we hope it'll bring in a few jobs and give an economic boost when guests go out to the pub and use the local shop. Surely it's a win all around?'

'I agree with you, boy but I can't say too much because everyone knows I'll make a few bob out of it.'

'Any clue what might help to convince them we'll be a real asset?' Ashley's intervention took him by surprise. 'We sure would appreciate you helpin' us out.' Her smile brightened. 'Isn't this when you Brits sit down and have a cup of tea?'

'I never turn down a cuppa but don't offer me any biscuits.' Yeatman ruefully patted his round belly. 'The wife's got me on a diet and she'll skin me if she catches me cheating.'

'We sure don't want that. I promise no biscuits or cookies.' Ashley started to fill the kettle. 'Let's put our heads together and work out how to win over the good folks of Polgarth.'

Chapter Eight

Nessa had expected it to be even more chaotic than a normal Saturday in late June as she tried to juggle her routine jobs with her sister and reluctant nephew in tow, including preparing for three new families to arrive by mid-afternoon, but instead she was fighting off a lingering hangover and having a surprisingly good time. Last night Lowena packed her protesting son off to bed at nine o'clock before they polished off an inordinate quantity of wine and talked until the early hours of the morning.

The unexpected sound of Kit's boyish laughter mixed with Crispin's deep, rumbling tones drifted down the stairs. For someone who retreated from interacting with adults whenever possible, he didn't have the same problem around young people. Maybe it helped that Kit was a typical teenager wrapped up in his own problems and didn't ask the sort of awkward questions his parents might venture about the ex-soldier's past. When Crispin offered to help with painting her parents' old bedroom, he'd suggested they would do fine without supervision so Nessa and Lowena left them to it.

'Shall we give them a break?'

Her sister stopped in the middle of chopping bacon for a quiche and wiped a hand over her hot, shiny face. 'Good idea. I'm sure they'd be glad of a cold drink and I'm dying for one. I know this incredible weather is good for the visitors but I can't wait for it to cool off.'

Nessa yelled up the stairs but before she had a chance

to get their drinks, Polly bustled in waving a bright yellow leaflet in the air.

'I've just come back from the village. Look at this.' She shoved the flyer in Nessa's hand. 'They're stuck up all over the village.'

"PLEASE JOIN US AT TREGERETH HOUSE
FOR A FREE AMERICAN INDEPENDENCE DAY
BARBECUE ON SUNDAY 4 JULY FROM 4–8 PM.
ALL ARE WELCOME!"

'Benjy at the pub says it's a con to make sure no one opposes the planning application. We'll have to go.'

Nessa's heart sank. 'Me? Oh no.'

'You could come too.' Polly fixed her gaze on Lowena. 'Safety in numbers.'

'That's an excellent idea.' Her sister's eyes gleamed. 'I'd like to check out the opposition and meet this infamous American.'

Two sets of heavy footsteps pounded down the stairs and Kit stumbled into the room to slap his hand on the table. He swung around and grinned at his painting partner who'd followed as far as the door. 'You're slow.'

The closest thing she'd ever seen to a smile crept across Crispin's swarthy face.

'It's what happens when you get old and decrepit.'

Nessa hadn't heard him crack a joke before either.

'I'm starved.' Kit delved into the biscuit tin and dumped out a bag of Kit Kats on the table.

'I bet you like real American hamburgers?' Polly pushed the leaflet towards him.

'I 'spose.'

'We can all go together.'

Nessa did her best to ignore them. 'Crispin, come and sit down with us. You'll have to fight Kit for a biscuit before he eats them all.'

'Uh no thanks. I'm good.' He backed up a couple of steps.

'You must need a drink?'

'I'll take a glass of water if there's one going and get back to work.'

People shouldn't be forced into things. Her family would do well to remember that.

'I'm not sure this is a good idea.' Ashley tugged her grey cardigan in around her.

'The walk will do us good and it's just for a drink.' Ward tried to reassure her. 'Look at it as research into the local area.'

'Fine. We'll go if you're that keen.'

They strolled along Penmeor Road and he enjoyed her surprise when she spotted the sea in the distance. Apart from a couple of vacations to Florida – combining trips to the beach with the mandatory visits to Disney World – neither of them had any experience of being this close to the coast. As they turned on Primrose Lane a sharp memory of walking along here with Nessa haunted him.

'This is the beginning of the village proper and The Chough is just down there.' He pointed to the low whitewashed building jutting out on the right-hand side of the narrow street.

'I expected gift shops full of tat and cutesy tea rooms.'

Ashley sounded mildly disappointed at the straggle of cottages and sparse selection of businesses.

'You won't find that here. The Polgarth Valley is largely undeveloped and it's not close enough to the beaches for most vacationers.'

'Then why sink all your money into Tregereth? You really think folks are gonna come?' She ground to a sudden halt. 'Oh, for heaven's sake tell me you didn't?'

'Didn't what?'

'Plan all this to lure me away from Bunny.'

Ward felt his face burn. 'I admit when Peter Endean raised the possibility of turning the house into a business you did pop into my head but I needed a new challenge.' He shrugged. 'If it helps us both, what's wrong with that?'

'Nothing I suppose but why don't you consider getting back into the music business as a solo artist or even on the management side like Dad swapped over to doing?'

'No.' The curt response made her flinch. If he apologised it could ignite a conversation he was determined to avoid. 'We're here.' Ward opened the door and stood back to let her enter.

'Oh wow, now this is awesome. It's exactly how I picture a proper English pub.' Her face lit up. 'Thanks.'

'What for?'

'Dragging me down here.' She stood on tiptoe and kissed his cheek. 'I'm glad I came.'

'Me too.' Ward ruffled her spiky red hair. 'Let's get a drink.' He steered her towards the bar, idly gazing around to see who he might know. At the back of the room by the fireplace, Polly and Jack sat next to each other at a small round table eating a meal. Her knife froze in mid-air as she glared at him.

'Why is that odd-looking little woman with the blue hair looking daggers at you?'

'Tell you in a minute.' Once they were settled at a table well away from the Greens he gulped down half of his beer and swiped a hand over his mouth.

'Is she anti-American?'

'Nope.' Ashley wouldn't shut up until he came up with a feasible story. 'They live year-round at the campsite where I stayed before I moved into the house.'

'Okay, so what'd you do to rile her up?' She smirked. 'There's a woman involved isn't there?' Her expression softened. 'That's good news. You deserve someone decent after that cow Sophia.'

'It's nothing. Might have been but ... didn't work out.'

'So where does the mystery woman live?'

Ward heaved a sigh. 'Her property borders the field where I'm gonna put our yurts.'

'Oh my God, she's the Cornish version of the girl next door.'

'Can we please change the subject?' He gritted his teeth.

'Name.'

'Sorry?'

'What's her name?' Ashley rolled her eyes. 'This is a small place and I don't wanna put my foot in it if I bump into your discarded girlfriend.'

'Her name's Nessa Vivian but she wasn't my girlfriend and I didn't discard her.'

'Oh, wow *she* dumped *you*, didn't she? Doesn't she know who you are – or were?'

'She knows *nothing* about my Nashville life.' Even in the heady days of being a household name he'd been disdainful of people who wouldn't have given him the time of day if he'd been waiting tables while he scrabbled around for a record deal. He'd luckily not been in that situation because his father's connections smoothed his pathway but it didn't change the wrongness of it. 'There was no dumping involved because we never even went on a date. Whatever it might've been ended when she found out I'd be in direct competition with her business a few hundred yards up the road.' He shrugged. 'Well that's the way she saw it. I tried to reason with her but ...' Ward stared down at the table and ran his fingers over an indecipherable name scratched in the old wood.

'I'm sorry.' Ashley touched his hand. 'We're a useless pair.' A determined gleam burned in her eyes. 'Drink up! We've got work to do. Now we've got a reluctant Cornishwoman to win over along with the rest of the village.'

He dredged up the semblance of a smile and knocked back the rest of his pint. It was worth putting up with her enthusiasm for setting his life straight if it took her mind off worrying about her jerk of a husband for a while.

Chapter Nine

Nessa smoothed down the crisp blue and white cotton dress Lowena had plucked from her limited wardrobe and insisted she wore to the dreaded barbecue. She'd stuck to her guns for the last week swearing nothing and no one would drag her to Tregereth today. It worked until her sister and Kit turned up yesterday to help paint another bedroom – again minus Antony.

'If you don't mind we'll stay the night then I can help you sort more of Mum and Dad's stuff in the morning. If we make do with a sandwich lunch while we're working we can eat later at Ward's barbecue.'

Game, set and match to Lowena.

'I assume you're going to do something with your face?' Her sister eyed her up and down. 'I'll be in the kitchen with Kit when you're ready.'

Nessa reluctantly pulled out the make-up she reserved for special occasions, surprised it hadn't all dried up through lack of use. A few minutes later she examined herself in the mirror and almost wiped it all off. Remembering the gleam of appreciation in Ward's eyes that day in the orchard was the only thing that stopped her.

'Right, that's me ready ... oh hello Polly. Jack.' Wary glances flitted between the three of them when she strolled into the kitchen. Kit was nowhere to be seen. Presumably he'd been banished from whatever secretive conversation was going on.

'You're aren't going to like this, lovey but you need to

hear it.' Polly shook her head. 'We went down the pub last night for a meal and Ward came in with a woman.' She practically spat out the last word. 'Small, skinny little thing she was with red hair straight out of a bottle. Not a patch on you. They were all smiley and touching each other. Benjy overheard George Yeatman say she's an old friend of Ward's sister come to work with him on Tregereth House.' She scoffed. 'Like anyone believes that.'

'I don't know why not and anyway he's free to do what he wants.' If that was the truth why did she feel so miserable all of a sudden? She'd come to the conclusion she might've overreacted to his development plans, leaving a door open to exploring the attraction simmering between them. This piece of unwelcome news put paid to her ridiculous idea. 'Are we all set?'

'You still want to go?' Lowena's jaw dropped.

No matter how much it might hurt to see him with another woman she refused to be the object of anyone's pity. 'Of course.' She shooed everyone outside and stuck a note on the door telling the campers she'd be back by seven o'clock if they had any problems.

The closer they came to Tregereth the lower her spirits sank.

'Are you sure this was a good idea, Ash?' Ward frowned at the platters of hamburgers and hot dogs waiting to be cooked.

'Don't be so negative.'

She'd thrown herself whole-heartedly into the project, tracked down red, white and blue bunting, balloons and American flags and even made the hamburgers from scratch because she couldn't find any at the shops to satisfy her discriminating tastes. The idea for a Fourth of July barbecue came about while she and George Yeatman were poring over plans and fine-tuning the pre-application submission for the local council. One thing the planning case officer would discuss was how to draw the local community into their ideas so there wouldn't be any backlash when the final plan was submitted.

'How many folks are we expecting?'

Ashley's smile widened. 'Who knows? I stuck flyers up around the village and George is roundin' up all his family and friends. He's convinced people will be too curious not to come.' She squeezed his arm. 'Come on, it's time you were on grill duty.'

'Yes ma'am'.

'You're the best brother a girl could ask for.' She rested her head against his shoulder.

'I haven't always been. I should've—'

'Shush.' The animation and good humour seeped from her face. 'Don't ruin things today.'

Ward wasn't dumb enough to believe Bunny Radnor would let his wife fade out of his life without a fight. They were living on borrowed time because sooner or later he'd track Ashley down and there'd be trouble. Big trouble.

'Fair enough.' He grabbed the tray of meat and headed outside.

Another beautiful sunny day combined with people's natural nosiness did the trick because soon he didn't have time to worry about anything other than whether they had enough food. The locals were lapping up the uniqueness of talking to two real live Americans and there was plenty of back-and-forth banter about Independence Day. So far all of the reactions were positive but he reminded himself to take that with a pinch of salt. There was a strong chance his detractors wouldn't turn up in fact he was pretty sure the main one wouldn't be seen dead anywhere near today's party.

During a brief lull he grabbed a beer from one of the ice-filled tubs and popped the top. He was mid-swallow when he glanced across the freshly mowed lawn and almost choked.

Nessa locked eyes with Ward and walked straight into Polly's back. He'd abandoned his usual black ill-fitting clothes for smart navy shorts and a red and white striped T-shirt, showing off lean toned muscles she could've done without seeing.

'Let's get something to eat.' Lowena poked her arm.

'No thanks. You go ahead if you want.' Before they arrived she'd planned what to say and how to act. Cool and polite. Now her face burned hotter than the smoking barbecues and her legs wobbled like unset jellies.

'That's her over by the drinks.' Polly jabbed her finger towards a young woman standing behind a folding wooden table set up under a large, shady oak. Ward had appeared to appreciate Nessa's curves but the woman in question didn't have an ounce of spare fat on her. 'I think it's only friendly to say hello and welcome her to Polgarth.'

'I can't. Take Lowena and Kit with you while I have a wander around.' She glued on a smile. 'You can be my reconnaissance team.' She left them to it and sidled

72

around the edge of the expansive lawn, avoiding talking to anyone. A sign by the open front door encouraged visitors to look around the house. Ward had a queue of people waiting for food so she should be safe if she popped inside.

Nessa glanced around the hall with a sinking heart. The elegant house would be very attractive to visitors when it was renovated. Other visitors were tramping around over her head so she decided to start with the downstairs and pushed open one of the four doors leading off the hall. She stepped into a long narrow room which she guessed was Henry Thomas's best parlour where he entertained his most important guests. The ornate ceiling and elaborate mouldings remained although the chandeliers that would've hung there were long gone and there were only a few sparse pieces of furniture scattered around.

'I hoped you wouldn't be able to stay away.'

She jerked around. Behind Ward's dark-rimmed glasses lurked a distinct wariness that overrode his hospitable smile. 'Seriously? Be honest for once.'

'I've never lied to you … we haven't swapped all of our secrets but that's not the same thing is it?'

Without answering, she stepped away and wandered over to an elegant walnut writing desk, positioned by the beautifully proportioned bay window to make the most of a sweeping view out over the garden. 'This is beautiful. Did it come with the house?'

'Yeah, there were a few bits left behind. Not many. Most of the original furniture is long gone.' He gave her a searching look. 'I'm sorry about what happened …'

A fleeting touch of annoyance crossed his face as Peter Endean strolled in from the hall. 'Have you come to make sure I haven't ripped the house apart yet?'

'Not at all.' Peter smiled at her. 'Good afternoon Nessa. Are you checking up on your competition?'

'I sure hope she doesn't see me that way.' Ward jumped in.

'I'm reserving judgement.'

'But if I'm successful won't it boost the whole local area?'

'Isn't that rather presumptuous of you?'

By his confused expression, Peter hadn't expected his innocuous remark to set off a verbal battle.

'I'll leave you both to it and head home. There's always work to do when you have a holiday business to run.' Nessa left the pointed remark hanging in the air and beat a swift retreat. She heaved a sigh of relief when she made her way back out of the front door without being accosted again. Heavy footsteps crunched on the gravel behind her and she expected to see one of the villagers.

'Hang on a sec, please. We need to talk.' Ward grabbed her arm. 'I ... there are things I need to say. I really wanted to introduce you to—'

'Your girlfriend? Seriously?' She pointedly stared at his hand until he let go.

'Ashley isn't my girlfriend.'

The quiet denial struck her hard and Nessa ached to believe him. 'Of course not. She's an old friend of your sister here to help get your business up and running.' Her air quotes made him cringe. 'That's the public explanation, right? Anyway it's none of my business.'

'But I want it to be.' His frustration was obvious. 'You were the one who decided we couldn't ... whatever.'

'I know that but maybe I thought you'd wait more than a few days before moving in a woman you must've had all lined up. Stupid of me really.' Tears pricked at her eyes but she wouldn't give him the satisfaction of letting them fall.

'I don't suppose there's any chance you'd believe me if I swear that's a load of garbage?' Ward's syrupy drawl thickened.

'Bingo.'

'I can't blame you.' His shoved a hand through his spiky hair. 'I can't explain today because it could hurt someone badly if it got out but one day I'll prove you wrong.'

'I won't hold my breath.' Nessa strode off without a backward glance. That didn't stop her sensing his disappointment all the way to her bones.

Chapter Ten

'Hey good news, kid.' Ward waved a letter at his sister. 'My visa has been approved.' It'd been a long, busy week since his attempt to make amends to Nessa at the barbecue was roundly rejected and this boost had arrived at the perfect time.

'Awesome.'

'You'll need one, too, later on – a simpler one than mine – but for the time bein' as long as I don't pay you we're good.'

'I guess board and lodging don't count?'

'You're family.' He half-smiled. 'Even if no one here knows it.'

'What's next?'

'I've got an appointment with a solicitor in Truro next week to see about registering the business and all the other legal details that need to be done.' Any day now he should hear back on the pre-planning application paperwork and then things should really get going. A brainwave struck him. 'You fancy seein' something more of Cornwall? The guys are starting on the roof today and George is comin' to keep an eye on them. We'll only be in the way.'

'What've you got in mind?'

'We could drive down around Redruth and check out where old Bill Tremayne started off life. Wheal Rosen doesn't exist any longer but we can look around the area and go down the Poldark Mine that's nearby because it's open to visitors.'

'I guess.'

'What's bothering you?' He received a scathing look telling him Ashley couldn't believe he'd asked such a dumb question. 'Sorry.'

The hint of amusement tweaked at her mouth. 'I know you are. You can't help putting your enormous feet in it when you try to be considerate.' Ashley slid him a sideways look. 'Is that what happened with the pretty brunette I spotted you trying to talk to at the barbecue last week? I could tell she wasn't having any of it and you came back with a face as long as a month of Sundays.'

'You sound so like Granny Spencer it's uncanny.' He chuckled. 'She had a bottomless fund of southern sayings you don't hear much any more.'

'I wish I remembered her better.' Sadness flickered over her face. 'I've only got a vague memory of goin' to visit her at the nursing home one time. I can't have been more than four or five. She had a tin with a picture of a black cat on it and it was full of—'

'Jelly beans.' Ward finished the sentence for her. 'Mom used to get mad at me because Granny was diabetic and not supposed to eat sweets but she'd bribe me to sneak them in for her.

'You think you're so clever distracting me, don't you?' She gave him another evil stare. 'This doesn't avoid you talkin' about Nessa.'

'How'd you find out her name?'

Ashley whooped a loud cheer. 'I didn't know for certain but you've confirmed it. When I was fixing your friendly realtor a drink at the barbecue he mentioned y'all meeting in the house and I got the impression the two of you were at loggerheads. Putting two and two together wasn't hard.'

'She thinks I'm out to destroy her business.'

'That's a reasonable supposition.' Ashley nudged his arm. 'I reckon she's got the hots for you though or it wouldn't bother her quite so much.'

Ward didn't respond.

'She looks a lot like Sophia.'

'Only on the surface thank goodness.'

'That's one point in her favour.'

No one in his family ever took to Sophia. They held their tongues when it was a simple business partnership – the number of gold and platinum discs and awards they won spoke for themselves – but when their relationship became personal and they moved in together, the gloves came off. He didn't pay attention to the warnings until it was almost too late. 'Forget it. Are we goin' out or not?'

'You don't think I'm safer stayin' here?'

'You'll be fine.' If he cracked a joke about Bunny not having any spies in Cornwall that would make things worse. 'No one's gonna hurt you while I'm around. I've done a lousy job of lookin' out for you but I've promised Dad ...' The words dried in his throat.

'Dad knows I'm here?' Ashley turned white. 'That means Mom does too and she's gullible where Bunny's concerned. You idiot. I can't believe you did that.'

'I didn't do it on purpose.' He explained how it happened but his sister's grim expression didn't alter.

'I'll have to leave.'

'Don't do anythin' rash. Listen to me a minute. Please.'

'Rash? You don't have a clue, do you?' Her voice turned shrill.

'Then tell me,' Ward pleaded. 'Tell me everything.' A flicker of indecision shadowed her face. 'Let's get out of here. We'll talk in the car.'

'Fine.'

'You might want to change into trainers for exploring the mine workings and grab a light jacket. It'll be chilly underground.'

'Be ready in five.'

After she disappeared upstairs he sat with his hands planted on the table, head bowed to get his emotions under control. If his sister's story was only half as bad as he imagined, how would he react when he came face to face with Bunny Radnor again?

Nessa leaned against the doorpost drinking her coffee and relished the brief rest from her endless to-do list. Her visitors were all out for the day making the most of the continuing sunshine and she longed to grab her swimsuit and head for the nearest beach too. Polly and Jack couldn't have been more enthusiastic when she let them in on the garden-to-table ideas so the three of them were working hard now to get the plans together. Polly kept bringing in samples of new recipes for Nessa to taste and Jack had a pilot two-day course sketched out. Now he was nagging her to get someone younger and more tech savvy on board to create a social media profile for the farm.

She spotted Crispin heading towards his tent and waved at him to come see her.

'Do you want me to get on with the painting? I could finish your bedroom today if you want.'

'That'd be great but could you take a look at the kitchen tap in "Mr Blue Sky" first? It's dripping.'

'No problem.' He shaded his face with his hand. 'How soon are you hoping to get this garden-to-table lark up and running?'

He tried to hide his dismay when she shared her plans because they both knew people were his worst nightmare or at least one of them. 'It'll be at least another month and possibly longer because I haven't even advertised yet and there's a lot more clearing out and redecorating to do. I really need en-suite bathrooms installed but I'll have to convince the guests it's all part of the authentic farmhouse experience until my bank account is healthier.' Her attempt at a joke didn't drag even the ghost of a smile from Crispin.

'I'll take a look at the leak.'

A sigh escaped her lips watching him walk away, hunched and despondent. Her phone dinged with a text message from Lowena.

Kit is headed your way on the bus. He's mad at me. College finished so OK if he stays a few days? He's got his tent. Put him to work.

After the barbecue they'd had another heart-to-heart chat and although she'd been forced to admit her brother-in-law's secretive behaviour was suspicious she still couldn't wrap her head around the idea that he was being unfaithful to her sister. The worst moment came when Kit cornered her and asked if she thought his parents were going to split up. Of course she denied anything was wrong but he'd obviously seen and heard enough to make him worry.

No problem.

A rusty, green Land Rover drove in and stopped next to her. Nessa plastered on her best smile as a dark-haired man jumped out. 'Good morning. Can I help you?'

'I hope so love. Do you have any caravans free?' He flashed a toothy grin. 'I'm guessing they're not free – you probably want people to pay for them.'

She picked up on his melodic Welsh accent. 'We're like that in Cornwall.'

'Typical.' The man stuck out his hand. 'Aled Jones. Lance-Corporal. Royal Welsh Regiment. I'm down from Cardiff for a week.'

Now the military bearing and regulation haircut made sense. 'You're in luck "Good Day Sunshine" isn't occupied.' He looked puzzled. 'I named my caravans after songs I like and that one's for Beatles lovers.'

'That'll do me then. How much is—'

'Sorry to interrupt Nessa but I need a couple of washers to …' Crispin stared at Aled and froze.

'Well I'll be damned. Old Cornflake. How are you hangin' mate?'

'You two know each other? Were you in the army together?' Her new guest smiled and nodded but poor Crispin looked as though he'd seen a ghost.

'We'll have to catch up later.' The Welshman grinned. 'How about a drink tonight? I want to hear what you've been up to.'

'I'm busy.' Crispin stalked off leaving her stranded and embarrassed. If she apologised for his rudeness that would make things worse. He was never the most sociable of men but this was out of character.

'Do you want to take a look at the caravan before we do the paperwork?' She'd noticed Aled following Crispin with his eyes but now he switched his attention back to her.

'Uh no I'm sure it'll be fine.'

Neither of them mentioned what just happened.

It was challenging to tackle Cornwall's roads and talk at the same time but Ward sensed it helped his sister not to have to look him in the eyes while they chatted.

'I guess I can use being seventeen and naïve when I met Bunny as an excuse for why I made the huge mistake of getting married so young. What does anyone know at eighteen about picking a partner for life?' Ashley sighed.

'You don't have to be a teenager to be dumb. I was a damn sight older but I still managed it.'

'We're a good pair.'

'True.' He flashed her a grin. 'Not very reassuring is it?'

'You might not believe me but I swear Bunny never laid a hand on me in anger.' The nervous way she flexed her long thin fingers told its own story.

'But he belittles you, Ash. He's sucked away your self-confidence. Cut you off from family and friends. Made you scared of your own shadow. That's not love. You know that don't you?'

'Yeah, yeah. You're right. Happy now.'

Ward took the sharp, spat out words as an encouraging sign that Bunny hadn't irreparably broken his sister's spirit. 'What made you leave him now? Because however you want to label it that's what you've done. You'd better not think of goin' back to the jerk either or you'll have me and Mom and Dad to contend with.'

'Look there's the sign for the Poldark Mine.' She pointed out of the window, clearly seeing their arrival as a reprieve.

If she thought they were returning to Tregereth House before hashing this out Ashley didn't understand him as well as he thought. He'd play along for now. 'Do you know anything about this place?'

'I've been a good girl and done my homework. I don't much fancy being underground but as we're treading in the footsteps of Bill Tremayne I'll suck one up for the team.'

It had only taken them half an hour to drive from Polgarth but this seemed a different world. The scarred, austere landscape was littered with the ruins of engine houses left by the failed mining industry and the sight called to something buried deep inside. He couldn't imagine how strange Tennessee must've been to a young man who'd grown up in a small hamlet only a couple of miles from where they stood now.

'This really gets to you doesn't it? If you aren't careful you'll write a song about it.'

'That's not happenin'.' He parked and jumped straight out. 'Come on.'

They joined the small group gathered around the entrance to the old mine but Ward had no interest in making idle chatter with strangers. He struggled to imagine ten-year-old Bill's trepidation the first day he followed his father down the mine. The guide led them towards a set of sturdy metal steps and as they started their descent the sense of being in another world clung to him. The dank, dark atmosphere with narrow tunnels barely tall enough for even a boy to stand up straight in closed in around Ward and against every instinct fragments of lyrics and music formed in his head.

'Why in heaven's name did Bill cross the Atlantic to do this same awful work?' Ashley's horror was clear. 'Why didn't he find a different job and stay here with his family?'

'Because jobs were scarce and mining was all he knew. It was in his blood.'

'Like music is in yours.'

He ignored her.

'Come on, let's get out of here. I'll be glad to see daylight again.'

If he was reckless enough to claim he'd seen far more clearly down here than he had done above ground in years, she'd call him nuts. 'Do you want to look around the industrial heritage museum or walk along the cliff path to see what's left of Wheal Rosen?'

'Not really. Maybe another day.' She pushed away a wisp of hair. 'I'm not up to talkin' any more either at least not the heart-ripping out sort.'

Ward followed her up the last flight of steps. 'I spotted a café when we arrived so I suggest we honour Bill and eat a pasty.' One snippet of information his sister shared in the car was Bunny's obsession with her weight. At first her husband convinced her it was all about her health but later she saw it as another sign of his need to control every aspect of her life. He sensed the compulsion to watch everything she ate with almost a religious fervour was a battle she'd fight for a long time. 'Deal?'

'Deal.'

He took that baby step forward as a good omen. Maybe it was a benchmark for his determination to woo Nessa all over again.

Chapter Eleven

'Mind if I tag along if you're headin' back to the farm?' Ward pushed off the wall outside the village shop. He'd thought hard after his revelations at the mine a couple of days ago and come to the conclusion the only way to have even a slim chance of winning over Nessa was complete honesty. He'd strolled down from the house to pick up a few things in Polgarth with a plan to drop into the farm on the way back. Instead he spotted Nessa chatting outside the pub to another young woman and loitered around until she finished and crossed back over to his side of the road. 'Let me take those.' He reached for her two canvas shopping bags.

'Why? Am I looking feeble today?'

'Of course not. You look …' *Yeah, that honesty plan lasted a long time*, he thought. If he said she looked so damn beautiful he wanted to wrap his arms around her and smother her with kisses she'd smack him. Her faded pink T-shirt and white shorts showed off work-toned arms and sun-kissed skin. With no make-up and her dark hair tugged back in a simple ponytail she could pass for a teenager but thankfully was all woman.

'Cat got your tongue?' Her teasing smile broke through.

'Uh do you fancy getting an ice cream?'

'You know I can't resist.'

That almost begged for a flirtatious comment in return but he held back, smiled and gestured towards the shop door. 'My treat.'

'I warn you I skipped lunch so it won't be a ladylike one scoop in a cup order.'

Ward chuckled. 'Good. Then I won't feel such a pig ordering the mammoth one you've got me hooked on.'

'Hello my 'andsome.' Fay Sampson hurried over to serve them and beamed at Nessa. 'You did me a big favour sending this one in 'ere.' She gestured at him. 'Almost eating me out of butterscotch ice cream he is.'

'Really?' Nessa's eyes sparkled. 'Happy to help. You can give us two of them today, Fay. He's paying.'

Soon they were back outside and he reminded her about his first question.

'It's a free country. I can't stop you walking on a public road.'

Ward fell into step alongside her. 'The weather sure is pretty.'

'Is that the best you can do for sparkling conversation?'

'I want to tell you a secret I haven't shared with anyone else here.'

'You sound like a five-year-old on the school playground.' Nessa scoffed at him.

'Ashley Radnor isn't an old friend of my sister.'

'Well, what a surprise.'

'You condemned me without asking for the truth.'

She stopped walking. 'If I'd asked would you have told me?'

'Probably not.' The admission made her smile. 'It's … tricky.' Ward steadied himself with a deep breath. 'So, Ashley is my younger sister.' He watched Nessa's eyes widen as he rattled off a brief explanation about her disintegrating marriage. 'She needs to lie low for a while.

One reason I dreamed up the project at Tregereth is to help her because the hospitality business is her thing.'

'It did strike me as odd. You seem an unlikely sort of person to think of running a tourist site.' Nessa tried to stifle a giggle. 'Sorry. That was rude.'

'Honest though.'

'How's the work going anyway?'

'Good. The new roof went on a couple of days ago and looks awesome. George and his helper started on the windows this morning and his electrician's coming tomorrow to see what needs doing and give me a quote.'

'And you're aiming to open next Easter?'

Ward nodded. 'Sooner would've been great but there's more to do than I bargained on I guess. The floors will be a massive job and we'll probably have a long wait for the bathroom fixtures Ashley's picked out.'

'She's getting into it then?'

'Oh yeah.' He smiled. 'This is absolutely her thing and it's cool to see her ... engaged and not brooding all the time.'

They finished their ice creams as they strolled through the gates of Pear Tree Farm. 'I know you're busy but is there any chance of continuing our conversation over a quick coffee?' He sensed her indecision.

'I ought to check on Kit first. He's staying with me while things are ... a bit difficult at home.' Nessa shrugged. 'He's not any trouble. I'd almost forgotten what a good kid he is underneath the surly teenager act. He used to love being out in the garden with me so I set him to work and he's practically taken over my vegetable patch.'

'Maybe he just needed to find something he really cared

about.' Ward held her gaze a moment too long, satisfied when a flush of heat blossomed over her face. It was hopeless. He couldn't resist this woman any more than an iron filing drawn to a magnet.

'There you are.' A stocky, bearded man approached them, stooped under the weight of an overstuffed backpack. 'I couldn't leave without saying goodbye.' He slid Ward a wary glance. 'Sorry. Didn't mean to—'

It wasn't hard to guess the stranger's identity even before Nessa introduced them. The elusive Crispin.

'Are you off to walk the coastal path?'

'No.' The man's grim expression turned to stone. 'I'm moving on. It's time.'

'I told you not to take any notice of my bossy sister,' Nessa chided him. 'It's nothing to do with her. I want you to stay and that's the end of it.'

'I wish it was.' Crispin's gruff voice throbbed with disappointment. 'Thanks for everything.' He shoved a hand through his shaggy hair. 'Maybe I'll be back one day. You know what they say about bad pennies turning up.'

Ward realised his presence was hindering the conversation. 'I ought to be goin', Nessa. How about dinner tonight if you don't have any other plans?'

'Oh okay.'

Even if she only accepted because she'd been distracted by the other man he didn't care. 'Pick you up at seven?' He nodded at Crispin. 'All the best pal.' Ward strode off, whistling to himself.

Despite a niggle of disappointment, Nessa appreciated Ward's thoughtfulness in leaving them alone. She noticed

Crispin giving nervous glances over his shoulder. 'Is this to do with Aled Jones?' All she got was a shrug. 'Come inside for a coffee before you go. Don't I deserve a proper explanation?' She'd lay a guilt trip on him if that's what it took to find out what was going on.

'Fine.'

'Come on.' She made a point of closing the door for once and hoped they wouldn't be interrupted. 'Sit down.'

Crispin slumped on the nearest chair. 'I'm sorry. I should've been honest when you first offered to let me stay. Nah that's wrong. I shouldn't have even asked but winter was setting in and …' His head drooped to his chest.

'You'd had enough.' Nessa abandoned filling up the kettle and sat next to him. 'I could see that and I'm glad you took refuge here.'

His dark, weary eyes fixed on her. 'I'm not the honourable army vet I implied I was. I went AWOL almost three years ago but I swear I didn't commit any crime apart from desertion. My last deployment tipped me over the edge. I was in a tricky relationship, drinking too much and couldn't handle any more crap. I left to survive.'

'Aled Jones knows about all this?'

Crispin nodded. 'We were good mates in Afghanistan. Went through a lot of the same shit together. These days the army doesn't always come after people like me but Aled will be obliged to report back that he's seen me and I can't take the risk.' His gaze slid towards the door. 'I can't be locked up. It'll kill me.'

'Where will you go?'

'I'm not sure and it's best you don't know anyway. That

way you don't have to lie if anyone asks.' He dragged himself to his feet. 'Don't bother with coffee.'

'Have you seen Polly and Jack?'

'I don't do goodbyes. I've had enough of the damn things to last a lifetime. You got a piece of paper and a pen?'

Nessa dug in her overflowing junk drawer and found an old Christmas card for him to write on the back of. She watched him scribble a few words and wished she could think of something to make him change his mind.

'That's my sister's address in Cardiff.' He handed her the card. 'I make sure she knows where to get hold of me in an emergency. If you ever need help get in touch with Rhonda.'

'And if *you're* in trouble you better bloody well come back here.'

Crispin's silent nod broke her heart. He hoisted his backpack on again and disappeared as fast as he'd arrived. Nessa stared out the kitchen window until the crunch of his footsteps on the gravel faded away.

'Maybe I should tag along and meet the delectable Nessa?'

Ward caught his sister's wicked smile.

'Don't worry I'm not goin' to spoil your romantic evening.' She smoothed the collar of his blue shirt and eyed him up and down. 'Gettin' you to ditch all those dark clothes was a genius move on my part and those pasties and ice creams are all helping. You don't look like a stick insect any longer.'

'Thanks ... at least I think so.' One of the first things

Ashley did was drag him into Truro and talk him into buying a bunch of new clothes.

'What's with the glasses anyway? You've never worn them before.'

'Old age. Comes to us all.'

'Hmm well another day we'll see about new frames. Those aren't very flattering.'

Sooner they got off that topic the better. 'Will you be okay here on your own?' A big eye roll came his way. 'Sorry. I don't mean to be—'

'My protective big brother?' She kissed his cheek. 'Off you go before I get sentimental. Neither of us wants that. Have fun.' Ashley shooed him away.

It couldn't be a prettier evening for a gentle stroll and he soaked up the view out over the green, undulating countryside. As soon as he knocked, Nessa flung open the door as if she'd been watching out for him.

Ward struggled not to gawk like a superfan faced with his favourite movie star. Nessa's floaty white dress was lifted from ordinary by a splash of flamboyant red poppies trailing down from one shoulder. Her dark hair was scooped up in a loose messy bun ripe for unravelling.

'Are you all right?'

Echoes of the first words she ever said to him filled his head. 'Yeah, fine.'

'So where're you taking me to eat? I'm starving. I've been too busy to stop for much all day.' Nessa patted her hips. 'They don't stay this way on fresh air you know.'

'Will The Chough be okay? It struck me as too nice an evening to drive anywhere.'

'I assume you've booked?'

'Uh no.' It hadn't occurred to him.

'I doubt we'll get a table. You might not believe it but they get really busy in the summer.'

Not a good start.

'I've got a couple of pizzas in the freezer and plenty of wine.' Nessa giggled. 'Don't worry the wine isn't in the freezer.'

'That's a relief. I was afraid it might be some odd Cornish habit.'

'We've got more than a few but that's not one of them.' She chuckled. 'So, are you taking me up on my offer?'

Ward kept to himself that he'd happily take her up on any damn offer. 'Pizza it is.' He followed her into the kitchen. 'Anything I can do to help?'

'Open the wine? It's only a cheap white plonk I'm afraid.'

'That's fine.' To make the most of the second chance she'd offered him he'd gulp down anything – even Coke – something all Americans were supposed to love but he couldn't stand.

She gave him a mischievous smile and passed over a chilled bottle from the fridge then rifled in a drawer for an opener. 'The glasses are in the cupboard to the right of the sink.'

By the time he fixed their drinks she'd ripped the plastic wrapping off a couple of pizzas and slid them on a tray in the oven to heat up.

'Cheers.' Ward raised his glass. 'To new beginnings.'

By her flushed cheeks Nessa caught the layered meanings behind the simple toast. No one would think he'd been an award-winning singer/songwriter because right now he was petrified of speaking in case he spoiled the moment with the wrong words. He longed more than anything to kiss her but was scared as a teenage boy on his first date. If he pushed too hard and too fast now he might ruin everything. All of a sudden she plucked the glass from his hand and set it on the table along with hers.

'Well?'

He became supremely aware of her light, floral scent and the warmth rising off her bare arms. Ward hoped he wasn't reading the challenge in her bright jade eyes the wrong way. He slipped one arm around her waist and pulled her close.

He tilted her face and with one sweep of her soft warm lips he was lost. Nessa's sharp intake of breath when he teased her mouth open and slipped inside forced him to slow down. 'What about the pizza?' Ward attempted to clear his head. Through the thin layer of cotton separating them he felt her thudding heartbeat.

'I'm happy to eat now if you want. It's your choice.' She puffed out a sigh. 'I'm rushing you aren't I?'

'Rushing *me*? *I* was thinkin' the same about *you*. In case you're wonderin' I got out of a bad relationship three years ago and haven't been with anyone since.' The thick rasp in his voice made her stare. 'No one's stirred me to take a chance again this way.'

'That sounds like an Abba song.' Nessa's mouth curled in a broad smile. 'I bet you're not a fan of them either?'

'Not really but the songwriter in me is deeply envious. People all around the world instantly recognise so many of their tunes and can sing along with every word. It's the ultimate accolade and …' Ward became aware of her intense stare.

'Songwriter? So that's part of your story. I wondered. I'll add it to the short list of things I know about you.'

He stroked her cheek. 'Is it enough to—'

'Want to do more than kiss you?' The shine in her eyes mesmerised him. 'Oh yes. Kit's eating with Polly and Jack tonight so we won't be disturbed. But first things first before we burn the kitchen down.' Nessa let go of him and grabbed a tea towel to yank the pizzas out of the oven. With a sultry laugh she slid right back into his arms and Ward tugged out one of her hair pins and followed it with the rest, dropping them carelessly on the floor. He tousled her hair around her shoulders and buried his face in the mass of silky waves.

'Come on.' She nodded towards the hall.

Ward followed her up the stairs and into a generous, square bedroom at the back of the house.

'We only finished painting yesterday so you'll have to excuse the smell.'

'Looks good.' The pale rose walls contrasted well with the old-fashioned dark furniture. 'You've got an awesome view.' They overlooked the walled garden and in the dusky twilight some of the lighter coloured flowers glowed. 'Of course this one's much better.' He turned back with a smile.

'My body suffers from too many pasties and not enough dedicated exercise.'

'Oh Nessa I'm no Greek god.'

'Thank goodness.'

She allowed him to peel off her dress but gulped a couple of sharp breaths when he reached to undo her bra.

'Okay?' As soon as she nodded Ward consigned the bra to the floor and cupped her lush breasts, making her shudder under his caressing fingers. He eased her white silk panties down over her hips then disposed of his own clothes in record time. 'You've no idea the hours I've spent thinking about this when I should've been selecting showerheads and bathroom taps. You're a very distracting woman.'

A satisfied smile inched over her face.

Ward tugged off the bed covers then reached for Nessa. He eased her down on the soft mattress before a brief flare of anxiety ran through him. But as he met her shining gaze and a heated flush crept over her lush body all his doubts disappeared.

Chapter Twelve

A yawn crept up on Nessa as she idly stroked Ward's bare back. Neither of them expected to end up in her bed last night although they'd both admitted to dreaming about it.

'I hate to say this sweetheart'—he stirred and blinked awake—'but ...'

'You need to go or Ashley will worry about you and you'll worry about her. Plus you've got the planning case officer coming by later.'

By midnight they'd been ravenous and sneaked down to the kitchen to bring back to bed a stack of thick ham sandwiches and mugs of tea. That stopped their stomachs rumbling and kept their hands otherwise occupied while they talked.

The solemnness returned to his pale grey eyes. 'You sure you're okay with my plans now?'

She'd arrived at an uneasy acceptance and agreed with him that they wouldn't be competing because different visitors wanted different things and could try to help each other out. It helped to talk through her own plans with him too and he had the bright idea of roping in Kit for help creating a website. 'It's not a problem. Honestly.'

Ward reached for his glasses on the bedside table and slipped them back on. 'Come up to mine for dinner tonight.'

'Will your sister be okay with me ... oh you know ... everything?' She trailed her fingers through his hair and wondered in the name of women everywhere why the flashes of silver feathering his temples were so appealing.

Nessa freaked every time she discovered a rogue grey hair and viciously attacked them with tweezers.

'Yeah. She'll be good. Ashley is equally curious about you.'

That was no surprise.

'All right if I come back around five to pick you up?'

'Perfect. I'll leave something here for Kit to eat. He's pretty self-sufficient.'

'I'd suggest you bring your toothbrush but I know you're kinda tied to this place.'

'You'll discover that's the downside to this business. You only get to take holidays in the winter when no one wants to come to Cornwall.' She gave a wry smile. 'You'd better get dressed Mr Spencer. We've both got work to do.' Nessa watched him tug on his clothes then Ward flopped back down next to her and drew her into his arms again, his dark, morning stubble scratching her skin. She tightened her grip around his neck for a long, lingering kiss. That would have to tide them over until later.

'This isn't an official promise one way or the other but from where I'm standing I can't see any real obstacles.' Julian Bullen tucked the papers back in his briefcase. The blunt council property case officer arrived on the dot of nine, refused Ward's offer of tea and made it clear he wanted to get on with the job not waste time with idle conversation. 'I hear you had a good turnout for your community party. The Cornish don't turn down free food.'

'You're not one yourself?' His ear wasn't yet tuned to the multitude of British accents and he'd discovered here in Cornwall there were all sorts – locals, incomers who'd moved from other parts of the country and tourists from all over the world.

'I'm almost as foreign as you.' Bullen's round serious face broke into an approximation of a smile. 'Lived in Birmingham all my life until I came here on holiday about five years ago. I met a Cornish girl and that was it.'

'Birmingham? I haven't ventured that far north yet but I've met a couple from your neck of the woods who only live a few minutes down the road. To me they sound different but that's probably because they've lived here for years.'

'What's their name?' Bullen chuckled. 'Listen to me. That's a daft question but I suppose if you came across someone else from Tennessee you'd say the same.'

'Sure I would. Their last name is Green. Polly and Jack Green.'

'Well bugger me.'

'You know them?'

'I should do. They're my aunt and uncle.' He scratched his chin. 'I suppose I can't blame them but they could've told us where they were to stop everyone worrying.'

By the time the whole story tumbled out, Ward guessed his visitor regretted ever opening his mouth. He got the distinct impression the other man couldn't wait to leave and crossed his fingers Bullen's next stop wouldn't be a certain pink camper van.

'Why're you looking so pleased with yourself?' Lowena's frown morphed into a satisfied smile. 'Oh my God you slept with Ward Spencer didn't you? Are you mad?'

Her sister broke with tradition and turned up for coffee

this morning, a Friday, ostensibly to check on Kit but more to discuss the state of her marriage. Antony was still sneaking around but continuing to deny anything was wrong.

'What about the red-headed woman? I'm not having you hurt and—'

'Shush. I won't be.' Nessa told her sister only as much as she needed to know. Ward had understood when she'd explained she couldn't hide who Ashley was from Lowena or Polly and Jack because they'd all think the worst of him – and her. She'd promised him on her life that none of them would spread the story around. 'Are you reassured now?'

'Yes and I'm envious.' Lowena sounded wistful. 'Not in a mean way. I haven't seen you this happy in ages and you deserve it. When are you seeing him again?'

'Tonight.' Her sister's eyes gleamed when she mentioned the dinner invitation.

'What're you wearing? You need something to impress his sister. Just because she wasn't terribly well dressed when we saw her, it doesn't do to be complacent. Come on. Upstairs.'

She trailed along behind and meekly allowed her to select an outfit from her meagre selection. So much for her vow to be more assertive.

'Assuming it goes well you need to invite him back here for dinner. I want to meet him properly.' A calculating look crossed Lowena's face. 'It's short notice but ask if he's free tomorrow because I'm incredibly busy next week. You could ask Polly and Jack too so he doesn't feel cornered. Kit could make up the numbers as he's still here.'

'He's being a big help.' Her nephew showed no sign of wanting to return home and she hadn't pushed.

'You're kind.'

'It's the truth.' Her sister must see the difference in her son. The morose, pale boy had morphed in the few short weeks since Truro College got out for the summer – breaking up earlier than most schools. He was now a tanned, contented young man. He worked hard, spending far more hours than she asked him to in the walled garden. When he wasn't busy digging she could find him at Jack's caravan where they had the new Pear Tree Farm website, Facebook page and Twitter account almost ready to launch. Most of the time, Kit even cooked for himself on a small camping stove. 'I think the independence is doing him good.'

'And being away from his parents arguing.' She scoffed. 'That's not accurate because Antony refuses to argue. He says I'm talking nonsense. That it's my middle-aged hormones and I'm simply paranoid. Then he walks away.'

Nessa didn't know what to say without making things worse.

'Forget that for now. Let me know as soon as you can if the dinner party is on tomorrow. I'm happy to bring the main if you rustle up a pudding.'

Dinner party? She didn't do "dinner parties" but there was no point arguing.

A few hours later she winced at her reflection in her mother's old Victorian full-length mirror. For two pins she'd rip off the ugly black dress. When she bought it for a Young Farmer's dinner with Jago Teague eight years ago it was sexy and form-fitting. An extra stone in weight later it showed every bulge and she could barely breathe. Lowena had fixed her hair in an elegant French pleat that didn't suit her. The patent shoes pinched her toes and their high heels were an accident waiting to happen. It flitted through her mind that tripping on the stairs and breaking her neck would be one way out of this ordeal. The sound of the doorbell left her no choice so she picked up her velvet clutch bag and headed down.

'Oh … wow.' Ward looked stunned.

'Blame Lowena. I've got the willpower of a flea when she orders me around. If you give me five minutes I'll change into something that's more me.'

'For heaven's sake don't.' His eyes twinkled. 'Poor Ash has dragged every item of clothing she brought with her on and off again all afternoon. She kept hunting me down to ask my opinion then not payin' the blindest bit of attention.'

'I see you weren't similarly affected.' His linen trousers and untucked navy cotton shirt were understated but struck the right note between smart and trying too hard. It made her happy that he'd abandoned the dark, loose clothes he used to hide behind.

'Nah. If you don't mind being seen with me let's go.'

For two pins she'd admit how yummy, handsome and kissable he looked but they didn't have time for what might ensue. 'For God's sake hold my hand or I'll topple over.'

Ward looped her arm through his and led her out to the car, holding the door open for her to clamber in.

'If I wasn't done up like a dog's dinner we could've walked up the road and enjoyed the gorgeous weather.'

'You, me and Ash must be the only ones lovin' the heat.' He chuckled. 'You're a rarity. Most folk here moan about it non-stop.'

'Ah but what you don't realise is that complaining about the weather is an ingrained British trait. It doesn't matter if it's hot, cold, rainy or a drought we'll be miserable about it.'

He jumped in next to her and reached across. 'If we walked I couldn't have done this.' A feather of searching fingers trailed up her thigh. 'Bingo.'

Nessa's cheeks blazed when he discovered the top of her stocking. Another contested addition that Lowena insisted upon.

'I'm gonna give your sister a big hug next time I see her.'

'That would be tomorrow.' She felt herself blush. 'I shouldn't take it for granted. Sorry. I expect you're busy.' Nessa cautiously explained the dinner party plan.

'Hey it's not a problem. I'd love to come. Nothing wrong with being taken for granted in the right sort of way. George and the young guy who works with him will be here again fixing the windows but they'll be done by about five.'

A momentary flash of nerves hit her as they turned into Tregereth. Ward parked in front of the house and the thin redhead she'd seen at the barbecue stepped out of the front door. Nessa considered it a major achievement that she managed to stumble from the car without falling face first on the gravel.

'Hiya, I'm Ash.' She pointed to Nessa's shoes and waggled one foot in the air, showing off her high-heeled silver sandal. 'Crazy minds think alike. My dear brother tried to warn me but I wouldn't listen.'

Their dresses were equally unflattering. His sister's grey satin cocktail dress hung off her petite angular figure and the dull colour drained her.

'Come in.'

Nessa followed her into the hall and laughed when Ashley prised off her shoes and swung them on her fingers.

'Feel free to follow suit. I'd offer to lend you some more comfortable clothes but ...' A deep flush zoomed up her thin neck.

'They'd fit as badly as this does.' The self-deprecating remark made Ward's sister laugh. 'There's no escaping the fact I'm a lot curvier than when I bought this dress. If you pour me a large enough glass of wine I might forget I'm in a straightjacket. I want to hear all about your plans for this place.' She sensed Ward's gratitude and started to relax.

Chapter Thirteen

Ward lounged on the patio soaking up another glorious morning. He relished clear days like this when the sea was visible in the distance from his new home. Home. The word rolled pleasantly around his mouth. He set down his coffee mug and gingerly picked up his guitar. Fragments of the tune that lodged in his head at the Poldark mine had slotted together like pieces of a jigsaw puzzle.

'Is this one of your secrets? You mentioned song writing but I'm guessing you performed too?' One of his shirts hung half way down Nessa's thighs and the sight of her tousled hair and naked face made his body tighten with remembered pleasure. Last night after dinner he talked her into ringing Polly to ask her to keep an eye on things at the farm. He'd picked up smothered giggles and a muttered conversation between the two women that he hoped equalled approval.

'You didn't check me out online? I thought everyone does these days?'

'I'd rather hear it from you.' She flopped down next to him.

'I told you my father is well known in the country music world and I hung around his studio growin' up, listening to him record and write songs.' Ward laid the guitar on the table. 'He gave me my first one of these on my eighth birthday and since then I never wanted to do anythin' else but make music. I did a business degree at college because my folks insisted I needed a back-up plan.' He felt his smile leech away. 'I started off as a solo artist but then my manager introduced me to Sophia. The Williams family were Nashville music royalty too and he had the idea we'd work well together. Duos are always popular and our styles clicked.'

'You clicked personally as well?'

'She was beautiful. Talented.'

'But?'

'Hard as nails. Ruthless. But it was all under a thick layer of southern charm so I didn't discover that until it was too late.' He shuddered. 'We started to rack up awards and hit records and our name recognition shot through the roof. I thought we had it all and asked her to move in with me but I'd blinded myself to problems that were obvious to everyone else.' He grasped Nessa's warm hand. 'She saw me as a stepping stone in her plans for an A-list solo career.'

'You became collateral damage?'

'We both did.' The shadows fell. 'We'd been sucked into the unhealthy celebrity lifestyle. That's a statement of fact not an excuse.' He needed her to know he accepted his share of the blame. 'My family rallied around to save me before things got out of hand but Sophia ended up in rehab. She got herself together for a while but it didn't last.' Ward exhaled a weary sigh. 'About eighteen months ago she was found dead and alone in a run-down motel.'

'An overdose?'

'Yeah. Bad heroin. Not that there's any other sort.' It wasn't hard to guess the question she didn't want to ask. 'I never touched that stuff.'

'It's inadequate to say sorry.' Her head nestled into his shoulder. 'You gave up music after that?'

'*It* gave *me* up until a couple of weeks ago. I tried my hand at all sorts of jobs since – everything from office manager at a landscaping company to selling swimming pools and hot tubs – but I was crap at them all so haven't settled to anything until now. Coming to Cornwall and finding this house … and you … has changed everything.'

'Would you play for me?'

He slipped the guitar back into his hands and haltingly strummed the introductory chords. Ward dragged out the story of a man torn an ocean away from the land he loves to help support the family who mean everything to him the only way he knows how and the last verse faded into the soft breeze as the man's ashes are strewn over the very earth he first mined.

'That's beautiful.' Nessa swiped a hand over her tear-glazed eyes then smoothed her damp fingers over his own wet cheeks. 'I bet there are Cornish folk groups who'd love to get their hands on that.'

'It's not for sale. It's too … personal.'

'Aren't the best songs always that way?'

The fact she was right changed nothing. 'I'm real pleased you and Ash hit it off.' Nessa's eyebrows knitted together at his abrupt turn in the conversation. 'Talk of the devil.' His sister hovered in the kitchen doorway, unsmiling. 'Come join us.'

'He's found me.'

No need to ask who she meant. Ward abruptly put his guitar down. 'How? There's no way Mom and Dad told Bunny anything.'

He prised Ashley's mobile from her shaking hands as she tried to pass it to him.

'They didn't need to. He's clever.'

Ward's anger grew as he scanned over the terse text.

Come home now or I'll be on the next plane to get you.

'He can't force you Ash. Take this to the police. Get a restraining order. File for divorce.'

She plucked at the hem of the shabby grey cardigan she hadn't worn in weeks and that he'd hoped was consigned to the bin. 'This was all a beautiful dream.' Ashley waved her hand around and heaved a distraught sigh. 'Deep down I knew that's all it could ever be. I've got some thinking to do.' She tipped her chin in the air and strode back inside the house.

'I could strangle him.' Ward slammed his fist on the table. 'What the hell am I gonna do?'

Nessa braced herself because he'd hate her answer. 'The absolute hardest thing. Nothing. We can't force other people to do what we think is best for them. Ashley needs to absolutely accept that his hold over her is wrong and choose to do something about it.' She slid over on his lap and kissed him on the mouth. 'I hate saying this too but I need to go home. Are you going to be okay?'

'Yeah.'

'Try to talk Ashley into coming with you tonight. It might do her good.' Nessa extricated herself from his embrace and stood up. 'Promise me you won't do anything rash.'

'I promise.' His weary agreement was the best she could hope for. 'I wish I could come with you now but I'd better hang around.'

They enjoyed another lingering kiss before she dragged

herself away. The glorious weather showed no sign of breaking although all the gloom mongers swore that would happen next week when the children all finished school for the summer holidays. Back at the farm she thought she'd better check on Kit and bumped into Polly outside the laundry.

'The wanderer returns.' Her friend couldn't stop grinning. 'I thought you'd moved in up the road. Are you off out with lover boy again tonight?'

'Actually, he's coming here for dinner. I'd love you and Jack to join us if you're not doing anything? Lowena's coming and I'll ask Kit as well. There's a chance Ward's sister will turn up too.'

'We'd love to.'

'I really appreciate you seeing to things here.'

'Anytime. If you're good with his business plans now then we are too and it's lovely to see you so happy.' The edges of Polly's smile flattened out. 'Has Crispin gone walkabout again? We noticed his tent is gone.'

She couldn't lie and Polly's face sagged when she heard the full story.

'Oh the poor lad. My Jack was right. He guessed something was up a long time ago and I told him not to be daft.'

'Have you met Aled Jones? I'm afraid I've been avoiding him. He's leaving tomorrow and I'm hoping to—'

'Ah Nessa, I hoped I'd catch you today.'

Her brain spun as she turned to face the Welshman. How much had he overheard of their conversation? 'Aled, it's good to see you again.' She avoided looking at Polly. 'I hope you're enjoying your stay?' He trotted out the standard answer about the wonderful weather and the interesting walks he'd been on.

'See you later love.' Polly scuttled off.

'I haven't seen old Cornflake again. Is he around?'

'Uh no. He's off hiking the coastal path I think.' Not exactly a lie because he could be for all she knew. 'He often disappears for a few days.'

The sunniness left him. 'So I get that it freaked him seeing me again but mates don't grass each other up. I know what the poor devil went through.' Aled opened his wallet and handed her a business card. 'If he gets in touch please try to persuade him to ring me. I might be able to smooth his path with the authorities. They won't want the trouble of prosecuting him.'

'You can't be sure.'

'Not a hundred percent but what's the alternative?' He shrugged. 'He lives like a hunted man for the rest of his life?'

'I'll do what I can.'

'I'll be off in the morning but I've had a great week.'

Nessa could still hear the pain in Crispin's voice when he spoke about being locked up. How was she supposed to care about what pudding to make for dinner tonight with that on her mind?

Chapter Fourteen

The meringues for the Pavlova resembled shoe leather, the cream refused to whip and the raspberries she'd relied on from her garden were tiny, scarce and far too sharp. Nessa had barely stopped all day. On top of all her normal tasks she'd given her house what her mother would laughingly call a lick and a promise and hoped it would be clean enough to fool her guests. That didn't include Lowena because nothing got past her sister.

She glanced at the clock and wiped her hands on a tea towel when the doorbell rang. With her guests due to arrive in a few minutes, the last thing she needed was a problem with one of the campers. Nessa plastered on a smile and opened the door to an unfamiliar middle-aged man with thinning mousy hair and a hangdog expression. 'I'm sorry but I don't have any vacancies at the moment.' A surprising position to be in but good news. The new website was already paying dividends and she could kick herself now for resisting the idea so long. She'd even plucked up the courage to speak to her bank manager. Again honesty proved the best policy and he'd been far more understanding than she'd expected when he heard about her plans.

'That's okay. I'm not looking for a place to stay.' An air of awkwardness hung around him. 'My name's Julian Bullen and I'm here to visit Polly and Jack Green.'

'Oh lovely.' She picked up on his Brummie accent and wondered what connection he had with her old friends. 'If you follow the gravel path up through the site, they are on the far right. You can't miss them as it's the bright pink one. In fact they should be ...' Nessa shaded her eyes against the early evening sun. 'There they are now on their way down here for dinner.' In the distance she heard the church clock strike seven and right on time Lowena's car swished in through the gate.

'Come and give me a hand with these hot dishes.' Her sister shouted out of the window.

Thankfully Ward strolled in from the road and she fell on him with relief. 'Would you mind helping Lowena with the food? Introduce yourself. I'm a bit tied up.' She caught the two men exchange nervous glances. 'Uh do you know each other?'

'Julian's my planning case officer up at Tregereth.' Ward looked wary.

Nessa didn't have a chance to interrogate him any further because her mystery guest broke out of his trance and stepped forward.

'Hello Aunt Polly. Uncle Jack.'

'Well bugger me. It's our little Jules all grown up.' Jack looked stunned for a second then turned with a broad smile, grabbing his wife's hand. 'Can you believe it? Isn't it great to see him again!'

'No, it's not and you know it.' Polly's faint voice was almost unrecognisable.

'I'll give your sister a hand.' Ward made himself scarce.

'Let's go inside.' Nessa herded them all into the hall. 'Jack, why don't you take Polly and Mr Bullen in the living room for a quiet chat?' She leaned back against the wall and sighed with relief when Jack steered them into what used to be her parents' best sitting room, all set now to be used by her garden-to-table visitors.

'What on earth was that all about?' Lowena grabbed her elbow and wheeled her into the kitchen.

'I've no idea. I'm afraid everything's behind schedule. My pavlova is a disaster and the table still needs to be laid.' Her sister wouldn't be able to resist coming to the rescue. She locked eyes with Ward. 'You can help me fetch more chairs from the dining room. We can't eat in there because it hasn't been cleared out yet.' When they were out of earshot of Lowena she cornered him. 'Make it quick. I want to know everything.'

'It's awkward. He asked me not to repeat what he told me.' He tugged off his glasses to polish the lenses and slipped them back on again.

'I don't care. Get on with it.'

Ward sighed. 'When Julian was at the house a couple of days ago we chatted some. He said he was from Birmingham originally and I happened to mention Polly and Jack. Poor guy looked like I hit him with a sledgehammer. Julian's their nephew.'

'I guessed that much when he called them aunt and uncle.'

'He reckons they left Birmingham after a ... family tragedy.'

'What sort of tragedy?'

'We lost our little boy in a house fire.' Jack pushed the door open and behind his shoulder she spotted Polly and Julian. Lowena was hovering at the back of the group, determined not to miss anything.

'Little boy?' Nessa was thoroughly confused. 'But I

thought you didn't have any—' She fell silent when Ward squeezed her hand.

'It were our fault.' Jack's eyes filled with tears. 'Poor Polly never got over it.'

'Neither did you my love.'

'I was only about ten at the time so I only heard bits and pieces until I got older.' Julian cleared his throat. 'A few years ago I suggested we try to find my aunt and uncle but Mum and Dad said to let it go.'

'Our families said some harsh things and we thought it best to leave. We know we did wrong but Danny was sleeping and should've been fine ...' Jack's raspy voice trailed away.

'He always tries to take the blame but it was my fault.' Polly bit back a sob. 'We couldn't afford a babysitter so I suggested taking a bottle of wine outside in the summerhouse for an hour. It was January and bitterly cold but we took a couple of blankets with us. We only had a glass or two but I was exhausted ... we both were I suppose and we fell asleep. When we woke up smoke was pouring out of the house.' She started to shake and Jack wrapped his arms around her. 'Jack tried to save our Danny but he had to be rescued by the fire brigade. I almost lost them both that night.'

'You poor souls.'

Nessa was surprised to see her sister's eyes glistening with tears.

'We've all done it. Struggled on until we were worn out and couldn't see or think straight.' Lowena's voice broke. 'You were unlucky.'

'They sure were,' Ward chimed in. 'That lamb is smellin'

mighty good. I reckon we could all do with a drink. Why don't we shift to the kitchen?' No one responded for a moment. 'You too, Julian.' He grabbed another chair and met Nessa's raised eyebrow with a shrug.

She couldn't come up with a better idea.

A whisper of the soft early morning air drifted in through the open window and Ward gathered Nessa back into his arms. 'Your sister's an interesting woman.' Last night he'd glimpsed beneath Lowena's starchy surface. 'Her support made a huge difference to Polly and Jack. What a burden they've hauled around all these years.'

'I'm playing devil's advocate here so don't think I'm getting at them but you can see where their families were coming from.'

It emerged over dinner that the police initially charged them with neglect but a sympathetic judge threw it out. He said the faulty electric fire couldn't have been anticipated although he did criticize them for not having a smoke detector and declared little Danny's death was a tragic accident.

'Yeah I get that but those are the very people who should've been holdin' them up.' He shook his head. 'Listen to me talk. We let Ashley moulder in her godawful marriage to that control freak because we didn't want to stick our noses in their private business.'

'But you're trying to put that right now.' She snuggled into his chest. 'That's all any of us can do when we make mistakes. I never got around to asking where Ashley was last night. Couldn't you persuade her to come?'

'No, she's a bit jumpy in company still. She was going

to call our dad for a chat and I hope he's persuaded her to stay a while longer.' He chuckled. 'I've gotta say your sister's a damn fine cook. That lamb was awesome.'

'It certainly was and her idea to turn my disastrous pavlova into an Eton Mess was genius. The raspberry liqueur worked miracles.' She frowned at the clock. 'Do you think I should wake her up?'

'I take it that was … unusual for her?'

'Unusual?' Nessa's grin exploded. 'Unheard of. A first. She put me to bed a few times back in my teenage days but I've never done the same for her.' Easing out of his arms she swung her legs over the side of the bed. 'I'll take her paracetamol and a glass of water while you go down and put the kettle on.' Her gaze danced over him. 'After you cover up your luscious bits.'

'Luscious bits? Never heard 'em described that way before.'

'There's a first time for everything.'

Including knowing you're in love, he thought. The knowledge blindsided him. It might be crazy to even think that way considering they'd only known each other a little over a month but perhaps dates on the calendar *were* simply numbers.

'Time to wake up sleepyhead.'

'Oh God please tell me that's not the time.' Lowena groaned at the clock and flopped back on the pillow, clutching her head in both hands. 'I should be at yoga.'

'Since when do you do yoga?'

'I started a couple of weeks ago. The doctor recommended it.' Two blobs of colour brightened her ashen cheeks. 'I saw him after Antony complained I was too uptight and needed to relax. It's another wasted attempt to save my marriage. Frankly I'm not sure why I'm even bothering.'

'Because you've made a life together for eighteen years and that's not something to throw away lightly.' Nessa held out the painkillers. 'Take these. Don't worry I rang Antony and explained you were spending the night because you had a couple glasses of wine and didn't want to risk driving home.'

'A couple of bottles would've been closer to the truth.' Her sister groaned. 'I doubt Antony missed me.'

She couldn't lie so said nothing. Her brother-in-law had sounded decidedly unconcerned.

'Thank goodness Kit wasn't there.'

'He had plans.' The fact they included holing up in his tent to avoid his mother was best left unsaid. 'Ward should have the kettle boiled by now.'

'He's a good man. Don't you dare let him slip away.'

'It's not that straightforward.'

'For heaven's sake you shouldn't expect it to be. You're not teenagers.' Lowena waved her away. 'I'll be down when I've freshened up and I'm vaguely presentable.'

That sounded more normal. She tried not to be too satisfied that for once she was able to help her sister instead of the other way around. Maybe the balance in their relationship could shift for the better. With a spring in her step she hurried downstairs and shimmied into the kitchen to treat Ward to the good morning kiss he deserved.

Chapter Fifteen

Ward paused in the middle of rolling pale grey paint on one of the bedroom walls and heard Ashley singing to herself as she scraped off old wallpaper next door. They'd avoided mentioning Bunny for the best part of a week since his threatening text but his shadow still hovered in the background. While they were waiting on the electrician and the plumber George had set them to work.

'You'll turn the paint rancid if you keep glowering at it.' Ashley materialised and leaned against the doorframe. 'You need a break and I've got the answer.' She flashed a satisfied smile. 'George reckons we should at least go ahead and select the yurts now because of the long waiting list. We'll need them early in the New Year so we can get them installed and furnished in time for Easter. Why don't you take Nessa up to London with you sometime next week to pick out what we need and stay overnight? I'll see to things here. Polly and Jack can manage the farm and keep an eye on Kit. It helps them to stay busy. I understand that.'

'Yeah I know you do.' Ward hated to see the pain filling her eyes. He couldn't get the harrowing conversation they had after he came home from the dinner party at Nessa's out of his head. When he told her about Polly and Jack's little boy, his sister crumpled in front of him and broke down in loud wrenching sobs. She finally confessed the real reason behind her abrupt decision to leave Bunny.

'I'm not trying to put myself in their shoes but I've got an inkling of what they've gone through. Bunny didn't tell me until after we married that he had no interest in having children and by then I was too afraid to argue with him. I'd already found out that if I did he'd give me the cold treatment for days until I apologised. I was always in the wrong. Never him.'

He'd wanted to comfort her then but hadn't dared.

'We slipped up somehow and I fell pregnant but I kept it to myself because I was terrified and happy at the same time if that makes sense. A few weeks later I suffered a miscarriage and it pushed me over the edge. That's when I knew I couldn't live that way any longer and called you.'

If Bunny Radnor had been in front of him then Ward wouldn't have been responsible for his actions. His brother-in-law's bullying behaviour had alienated her from family and friends leaving her marooned in a sea of loneliness and grief when she most needed support.

'So? Yurt shopping? Nessa?'

He forced out a smile. 'Yeah it's a great idea. I'll call and ask her but I know she's swamped at the farm so I'm not very hopeful.'

Ashley gave him a despairing look. 'Don't be dumb. It's harder for her to say no face to face. Smarten yourself up and dazzle her with your charm.' Her voice took on a wistful tone. 'The old Ward Spencer had that in spades.'

'Yeah well there's a lot I used to have. Life moves on.' He hammered the lid back on the paint can and set down the roller.

'I'll clean that for you.' His sister's gaze swept over him. 'Shower, shave and put on the cute blue shirt again. It worked last time.'

'Yes ma'am.'

Fifteen minutes later he presented himself for inspection before strolling off down the road. He couldn't imagine ever tiring of this overlooked part of Cornwall with its expansive views and what he'd call "soft" weather. The gentleness appealed to him. Of course he had regrets because who didn't if they'd lived at all but he was sure this move would never be one.

Even Nessa was tired of the interminable heat. Despite the downturn in bookings it would bring she longed for a return of Cornwall's more temperate weather with the occasional heavy shower during the daytime and cool breezes blowing in from the coast. She'd had to start watering her vegetables because they weren't getting enough rain. She pushed a sweaty lock of hair away from her face and kept digging.

'I guessed I might find you up here Miss Green Fingers.' Ward's tempting drawl thrummed against her neck and his wiry arms wrapped around her.

'I'm sticky and nasty.'

'Did I complain about that last time we were in bed?' His wicked chuckle sent her temperature soaring. 'There's a question I wanna ask and it's a yes/no answer. Don't quibble about details.' Ward swung her around for a kiss. 'Could this place survive without you for twenty-four hours?'

'If that's your question it's a daft one. How do you think I can—' Her protest morphed into a mumble when he kissed her.

'What did I say about details? Picture it. You. Me. A fancy London hotel.' Ward's eyes sparkled. 'Did I mention the chance to go yurt shopping in Croydon?'

'You certainly know how to entice a woman.'

'That's the plan. Ashley reckoned this would help.' He tugged at the blue shirt.

'Your sister's smart. I like her.'

'She likes you too. This outing was her idea. She reckoned we weren't givin' ourselves much of a break to … you know.' Ward looked bashful.

'The details you mentioned—'

'We'll sort them.' He glanced at his watch. 'I hate to kiss and run but I've got a hotel room to book.'

'We haven't agreed on a date yet.'

'Would Monday next week work? We can be back by Tuesday evening.'

Should she feel steamrollered or pleased to be wanted so badly? Secretly excited was more accurate. 'Hurry up with that kiss you promised or I might change my mind.'

'Nah you won't but I prefer to be on the safe side.' He swept her towards the ground as if they were dancing the tango and kissed Nessa breathless before setting her back on her feet.

'Off you go and do something useful.' Nessa shooed him away and hummed as she returned to attacking the weeds.

Ward found Ashley hunched over the kitchen table staring at her mobile. 'Everything okay? I don't remember giving permission for you to slack off while I was out.' His joke didn't dent in her stony expression.

'Dad called.'

'And?' He registered her tear-stained face. 'I'm not gonna want to hear this am I?'

'Bunny's been pesterin' them with phone calls and emails for weeks but they didn't say anythin' because they didn't want me to fret. Today he turned up on the doorstep and refused to leave until Daddy let him in.'

The dregs of his good mood evaporated.

'He made veiled threats. Nothing they could report to the police because he's a jerk but he's not dumb.' Ashley slumped further down into the chair. 'If I ask for a divorce he's gonna make y'all pay.'

'How? He's just tryin' to rattle you.' He squeezed her shoulder. 'I meant what I said. He's not gonna lay a finger on you while I'm around. You're safe here.'

'I know you'll try your damnedest but I can't live in fear this way. I'll be watching over my shoulder all the time.'

'But that's what you've done for the last ten years. Only difference is he's not breathin' down your neck any longer.' He felt his cheeks heat. 'Sorry that was too—'

'Blunt?' The sliver of a smile lightened her grim expression. 'I can't let him win can I?' Ashley stood up. 'If I don't get back to work my mean boss will hang me out to dry.'

'He sure will.' He couldn't sit around and wait for Bunny to make his next move. 'I'll be up in a few minutes.' Ward forced his smile back on. 'Hotel rooms don't book themselves.'

'Nessa said yes?'

'Of course. The Spencer charm worked its magic.' She didn't need to know he'd already booked the hotel. This far more urgent call was to someone who owed him a favour.

Chapter Sixteen

'Are you sure you don't mind?' Nessa was on edge. It seemed selfish to run off to London on a whim.

'For heaven's sake girl don't be daft.' Jack patted her arm. 'We'll be fine.' He'd pinned a notice to her front door diverting anyone with questions to them. 'And the boy will do as he's told or I'll ring up his mum to come take him away.' He nodded at Kit. 'You've left him plenty to do in the garden and we've got some website changes to make.'

'Don't you dare slip in any extra garden-to-table courses. Having four set up from mid-September is the most I can manage. That gives me a good six weeks to prepare and I need it. You know with the schools out we're into silly season here so the site's taking up a lot more of my time. If the courses are a success we'll start them again in the spring.'

'Yes boss.' Jack chuckled. 'Romeo's arrived.'

Ward's little blue car swept in through the gate sending gravel flying when he slammed on the brakes to jump out.

'Someone's keen.' Kit snickered.

'Mornin' gorgeous. You ready to get out of Dodge and have some fun?' Ward pressed a hard kiss on her mouth. 'Are these pair givin' you a hard time?'

Nessa wriggled away and thrust her overnight bag at him. 'Let's go or we'll miss the train.'

'Yes ma'am.' He steered her towards the car while she tried to issue more last-minute instructions. 'In you jump.'

Nervous tension kept its grip on her while they drove to St. Austell, boarded the train and settled into their reserved seats.

'First class? You must have money to burn.' Nessa watched his face fall. 'Sorry. I don't mean to be unappreciative. I've been a bit frazzled and you caught the brunt of it. I'd already had a go at Jack and Kit.'

'I thought I saw relief plastered all over their faces when we drove out.' He slipped his arm around her shoulder and she settled against his warm body.

'I haven't been on a train in years. Why don't you tell me about the yurt company? Are we going there this afternoon?'

'Yep, it's in Croydon and so is our hotel. We're gonna be extravagant and get a taxi from Paddington then we'll check in and have a bite of lunch before our appointment. The company keeps a yurt set up year-round so we can have a good look at that and talk to the guy in charge.' Ward's tempting grin returned. 'After that we'll be free until our train back tomorrow afternoon.'

She lowered her voice to a whisper. 'And what will we do to fill the time?' It shouldn't please her so much to see his face turn beet red.

Ward was thankful he'd studied up on the history and construction of Mongolian yurts so he hopefully didn't come across as too ignorant but he still experienced a slight wobble at the sight of the magnificent structure in front of him with its ornate traditional decoration. George Yeatman assured him it'd be a cinch to build the wooden bases the company recommended for the yurt to stand on and erecting them wouldn't be too challenging if they pulled in some extra help.

'It's beautiful.' Nessa traced her fingers over the swirling pattern painted on the canvas. 'You could have a Cornish Celtic design. That's what I'd probably go for but I've shelved the idea for now and it's not because you're doing them or the expense. My other new ventures will keep me busy enough.'

'Yeah they will. What do you think of this?' He pulled out the notebook he'd gone back to carrying and showed her the doodle he made combining a miner's pickaxe with a dark red rose. 'Bill Tremayne worked at Wheal Rosen near Redruth. The mine was named after the owner's wife and is the Cornish word for rose.'

'You've got a mile-long sentimental streak running right through you, Ward Spencer.' There was no hint of mockery in her gentle voice. 'It's perfect.'

The company owner was hovering behind them so he tried to concentrate on the business in hand. 'How about we go in your office and talk details?' An hour later he'd taken the plunge although he'd wobbled on placing the order. As soon as his planning permission came through – and he refused to believe it would be turned down – they'd go ahead.

'I reckon we need to celebrate.' Ward couldn't contain his excitement. 'Our taxi should be there by now.' He made short work of saying goodbye and whisked Nessa outside.

'Are we celebrating with a fancy meal and champagne?'

'Yeah if you like … after. I reckon that luxurious king size bed needs testing first.'

'Oh, do you?' She swept him a coy look through her dark lashes.

'Any objection?' Nessa turned pink. 'I'll take that as a no.'

In the taxi he noticed her peering out of the window and kicked himself for being selfish. On the train Nessa admitted she'd only been to London once before, on a school trip.

'Do you fancy goin' into the city for some sightseeing?'

'You said that with a straight face.'

'I meant it.' Her eyes narrowed, a sure hint that she wasn't convinced.

'We'll save that for another time ... I hope there will be others?'

'There sure will be. As many as you like.' Ward threw too much money at the driver when they pulled up outside the hotel and hurried Nessa out of the car. 'We're gonna talk before anything.' Her downturned expression made him laugh. 'Not for too long I promise.'

When they checked-in earlier they only had time to toss their bags on the floor and use the bathroom but now he gave himself a pat on the back for choosing this premium suite with its spectacular view over Wandle Park, a twenty-one-acre park with a river running through the middle of it.

'Wow this is quite something.' Nessa pressed her face against the window. 'I suppose I'm ignorant but I didn't expect to see this much green space close to London.' She looked abashed. 'Obviously Cornwall doesn't have rights over it all.'

'You'd enjoy seeing more of the world.' His simple

statement made her stare for a second before she gave him a sharp nod. 'Nothing to be ashamed of.'

'I know.' She turned back to face him. 'You never say much about Tennessee. Won't you miss it?'

Ward planted both hands on her shoulders. 'Is it cards on the table time?' Panic flitted across her face. 'I love Tennessee and I love my folks but I've told you some of why I came here in the first place. At the end of the day though those things haven't persuaded me to stay.' He fingered a lock of her silky dark hair. 'Aren't you gonna ask me the main reason I'm so keen on hangin' around Cornwall ... or have you guessed?' His heart raced.

Nessa watched disappointment bloom in his pale, intense eyes when she hesitated. 'I'm afraid to say.' That brought back his captivating smile.

'You and me both. Doesn't that strike you as awesome?'

She wasn't certain she'd describe her see-sawing emotions over the last couple of months that way.

'Hey we've both survived teenage crushes and a whole lot more to get this far.' Ward cradled her face and his warm thumbs strummed her skin like his beloved guitar. 'I'm guessin' one of the reasons you work non-stop is to keep everythin' else at bay. You've got your sister's family, Polly and Jack but at the end of the day you're alone too like me.'

That made it sound as if they were both desperate. 'I haven't thrown myself at you so I won't be lonely.'

'That's not the way I meant it.' His face dropped. 'Timing and intuition where women are concerned aren't my strong point. No wonder Sophia laughed when I asked her to marry me.'

'I didn't know you proposed?'

He turned bright red.

'She shouldn't have laughed. That wasn't kind. There are ways to turn a man down without being cruel.'

'You speak from experience?' Ward tilted her a quizzical look.

If they were doing honesty she needed to step up. 'I only snapped at you because deep down I'm scared you might be right.' There. The truth was out and it wasn't pretty. 'I am lonely. You nailed it.' Nessa puffed out a breath. 'A couple of years ago I drifted into dating an old friend. He's a local farmer and we were … comfortable together. I almost settled for that.'

'I'm damn glad you didn't.' He drew her back into his arms and tilted her chin with one finger. 'You are too?'

She managed a nod.

'That proved you're not desperate.' His mouth tugged into a mischievous grin. 'I'm not clutching at straws either. Don't like to boast but—'

'You've had other offers.' His shy shrug made her laugh. 'So, were you about to make me one?' Nessa slapped her hand over her mouth. 'Oh God now it's my turn to put my foot in it. Please don't think I'm angling for a proposal.'

'Don't worry, you're not gettin' one.' The swift response sent a wave of inexplicable disappointment flooding through her. 'Not yet.' Ward wrapped her in a massive bear hug and lifted her off her feet. 'We've talked enough. For now.'

When he gestured towards the bed, Nessa smiled. For now was the equivalent of "later". Later she could handle.

Chapter Seventeen

'Wow, Polly must've been busy. The brass bell outside my door is shining.' Nessa hopped out as soon as they parked outside her house. 'I'll have to go away more often.'

'Anytime. Just say the word.' They were still laughing as they carried their bags inside but he noticed her face settle into a frown as she gazed around the kitchen. 'What's wrong? Everythin' looks tidy enough to me.'

'Too tidy.' She touched the gleaming copper kettle on top of the range. 'Polly's the sweetest person but cleaning isn't her thing either.' Next, the fridge was scrutinised. 'This stainless steel shows every finger mark but they're all gone.'

'Ah you're back.' Lowena hovered in the doorway. 'I've done a few bits around the house to make myself useful.'

'That wasn't necessary but thank you. Did you come to see Kit?'

'Yes, but … would you mind if we talked on our own?' She fixed Ward with a pointed stare.

'You can say anything you want in front of him. We don't have any secrets.'

A flicker of guilt pulled at him because that wasn't totally true.

Lowena sighed and reached for the kettle. 'I expect you're ready for a decent cuppa after the dreadful stuff they serve on the train.'

'We're fine thanks. They serve a proper afternoon tea in first class. It was awesome.' Nessa beamed.

He saw her sister's eyebrows shoot up but she didn't say anything – something he'd guess was a rare occurrence.

'Where do you want these, Mum?' Kit struggled into the kitchen carrying two matching blue leather suitcases stuffed to bursting point. Several other bags were slung around his shoulders. 'Hi, Aunt Nessa. Did you have a good time?'

'Yes it was great but what's going on?'

'Set everything down for a minute.' Lowena exhaled a deep sigh. 'I haven't had a chance to talk to your aunt yet.'

'Mum's left Dad.' The teenager's expression hardened. 'The bastard has a girlfriend who's only a couple of years older than me.'

'I should've thrown him out but I couldn't bear to remain in the house with all of our ... old life around me. Would you mind if I stay with you until I can ... think what to do next?' Her eyes were suspiciously shiny.

'Of course. As long as you want.' Nessa pulled her sister into a tight hug. 'You didn't need to ask.'

'How about I help Kit upstairs with your bags?' Ward's offer earned grateful looks from both women. The boy looked mutinous but Ward grabbed the two heavy cases, leaving Kit little choice but to gather up the other stuff and follow him out of the kitchen. 'Do you know where these are goin'?'

'Mum's old bedroom I s'pose. It's the first on the right.' Kit glowered. 'I'm staying out in my tent.'

'Don't blame you.' Ward hefted the cases through the door and set them at the foot of the single bed. 'It might not seem like it but don't lose sight of the fact your dad still loves you. That'll never change. Teenagers aren't the only ones who do dumb things – adults screw up too.'

'Don't I get a lecture about taking care of Mum and not being selfish?'

'Nah you're a decent kid so you know all that stuff but it still sucks.' Kit's expression was grim. 'We'll help now. It's not all on you.'

The boy dropped his head and muttered something that might've been a thank you.

'I've been stuck on a train for hours and could do with stretching my legs. Do you fancy walkin' into the village for an ice cream?'

'If you want.'

Not the last word in enthusiastic but he'd take it. The chance for the sisters to talk uninterrupted was the best he could offer at the moment. Downstairs he yelled in the direction of the kitchen that they were going out and steered the boy through the front door. 'Your aunt's got me hooked on the butterscotch flavour.' He grinned. 'She makes them add a flake and a dollop of clotted cream. Do you think she's tryin' to fatten me up?'

'Not exactly Schwarzenegger are you?'

Kit's fleeting touch of humour felt like a huge win.

They resorted to making tea because it gave them something to do while they eased into the tricky conversation her sister clearly didn't want to have.

'How did you find out?' Now she was swamped with guilt for doubting Lowena.

'It's so clichéd it's ridiculous. I found a receipt in his coat pocket for a diamond bracelet and when I challenged him Antony admitted the whole sorry mess.' She rubbed a biscuit between her fingers until it was reduced to a pile of crumbs. 'She's an intern in his office for God's sake. Blonde. Pretty. Young. Her real name's Charlotte but of course he calls her Charlie.' Anguish filled her voice. 'What on earth does a bright twenty-year-old girl at uni with her whole future in front of her see in a solid, shy middle-aged man? I don't get it.'

'A father figure. Power. Money.' The well-worn excuses were that for a very good reason. 'Maybe it's just a fling. A mid-life crisis.'

'I don't care if it is. If you think I'm welcoming him back with open arms if he comes pleading for forgiveness you're as stupid as he is. I still have some pride left despite his efforts to destroy it.'

This wasn't the time to mention their long marriage or Kit. Her sister was hurting and needed her unconditional love and comfort. 'We'll get through this together.'

'I feel sorry for Ward.' Lowena managed a weak smile. 'One romantic night away and the poor bloke is plunged into my domestic tragedy.' She gave Nessa a long stare. 'He came through though didn't he? Kit's been knocked sideways and I don't have anything left in me to help him.' The helpless gesture with her hands said it all.

'Ward's a good man.'

'You've waited a long time to find him.' Two circles of heat flared in her cheeks. 'I was wrong about Jago Teague. No one should "settle" for another person.'

'Is that what you did?'

'No, but Antony did. His friends were all pairing off but he was shy when it came to chatting girls up.' She pushed away a lank curl. 'He spotted me at a party given by mutual friends and got one of them to approach me. That was it really.'

'But you didn't have to rush into marriage. You're smart. You could've gone to uni and had a career first.'

'Maybe.' Lowena rested her shaking hands on the table. 'You'll think it's ridiculous but I fell head over heels in love when he spoke to me. He had the loveliest voice – still does. I couldn't believe he was single and interested in me.'

Not for the first time it struck her how differently people often saw themselves. To Nessa her sister was beautiful, smart and accomplished and miles away from an insecure woman grateful that a decent man paid attention to her. 'He must've thought the same about you.'

'I doubt it very much.'

Nessa wondered how to phrase her next question before deciding she couldn't ask it. Not yet.

'Don't worry I'm not planning to stay forever.'

'I wasn't—'

Lowena gave a wry smile. 'Good heavens I'll give us a week under the same roof before we're at each other's throats and that's being generous. We love each other but live together long-term? I'll take a few days to clear my head then make other arrangements. I've got money. You know that.' She scoffed. 'I'll show him he's made a big mistake.'

'If this gets ugly Kit will suffer.'

'And you think it'll do him good to see me humiliated? For us to beg and scrape for every penny his father deigns to share with us?'

'Of course not but—'

'Let's not discuss this any more today. If you don't mind I'm off to unpack.'

Nessa wished herself back in the gorgeous hotel with nothing more stressful to think about than the next time she and Ward could enjoy the huge fluffy bed. On cue his enticing southern drawl drifted in through the open window and Kit roared with laughter at something that'd been said. Feeling sorry for Lowena didn't mean she'd sit back and let his warring parents rip her precious nephew's life apart.

Chapter Eighteen

'Hey great news.' A beaming Ashley thrust her mobile at Ward. 'Listen to Bunny's message.'

It was a stretch to link the words "great news" and "Bunny" but he attempted to trust his sister. His brother-in-law's thick drawl hummed down the phone short and to the point. If she wanted a divorce he wouldn't stand in her way. 'Awesome. You gonna get in touch with an attorney?'

'I already did yesterday while you were off gallivanting in London.'

'It was business remember.' A prickle of heat crept up his neck. 'Partly. I signed on the dotted line and as soon I let them know we've got planning permission they'll put the order in.'

'Oh Lord I can't believe I forgot.' She groaned and smacked her head.

'What're you gettin' at?'

'Julian Bullen stopped by last night.' She swiped a piece of paper from the kitchen counter. 'Ta-da! We're now official. Nothin' stoppin' us now. The Spencer siblings are in business.' Ashley wagged a finger in his face. 'This doesn't mean that long-term you aren't goin' to get back into music even if I have to kick your ass.' Her smile fell away. 'Doesn't it strike you odd that Bunny would give up this easily?'

The abrupt U-turn caught him out. 'I guess he came to his senses.'

'Maybe.'

'Have you told Mom and Dad the good news?'

'Yeah. They were thrilled although it was a bit odd because Dad started to say somethin' then shut up. I couldn't get him to finish it for anythin'.' She picked at a hangnail. 'Do you have anythin' to do with Micky Roper these days?'

'Roper? Why do you ask? I haven't seen him in years.' That wasn't a lie. Face to face he hadn't.

'Maybe not but you're a lousy liar all the same. What was it – a quiet email or a quick phone call?' Ashley shook her head. 'The two of you were best buddies. Did your thuggish friend plaster Bunny up against a wall for a "quiet word"?'

'Hey he's not a bouncer who chucks out drunks on Second Avenue. He owns a successful security firm.' Micky was also about three hundred pounds of solid muscle, a detail his sister plainly hadn't forgotten.

'So you're not denying it?'

Ward gritted his teeth and said nothing.

'Maybe I should be grateful—'

'I don't need your gratitude. I want you safe and out of this crappy marriage. Anythin' wrong with that?'

'No.' Ashley's voice turned cold. 'I totally get you meant well but check with me first next time. I'm not about to swap one loss of independence for another.'

'I know and I'm sorry.' He risked a fleeting smile. 'Worked though didn't it?'

'I suppose. Now I want to hear about your sneaky trip away but skip the gruesome details and stick to the business stuff.'

'There wasn't anythin' gruesome about it.' His good-humoured protest made her grin and soon they were both in fits of laughter.

Nessa let the muddy water swirl down the sink and she dumped the freshly scrubbed new potatoes in a saucepan. She had given Lowena the job of cleaning the two empty caravans before new visitors arrived and had hoped to have a good long chat to Ward while her sister was out of the way. Their conversation had turned out to be frustratingly brief because his planning permission had come through and he was tied up with George Yeatman all day. She wiped her hands on the tea towel and tapped out a quick text.

You. Me. Wine. The orchard. 9pm?

A smiley face and thumbs up emojis flashed back at her.

'It's only me. All right to come in?'

'Of course, Polly.' Normally her friend took the open front door as a standing invitation but there'd been an uncomfortable distance between them since Julian Bullen's visit. 'Have you got time for a coffee?'

'Madam isn't here?'

'Lowena's cleaning "Good Day Sunshine" and "Summer Nights".'

'I know.' She snorted. 'I could smell the bleach from our place.' Polly settled down in her usual chair facing the window. 'Jack and Kit are tinkering around with the website again and setting up an Instagram account then I think they're going to give the site showers a good scrub.' Her face softened. 'This is doing them both a world of good.'

She plonked two mugs down on the table. 'You aren't

sleeping well?' Polly's skin was grey, and new, deep lines were etched around her mouth.

'If I'm stupid enough to close my eyes I see our Danny's sweet little face. Not that I've ever forgotten him but he's there now ... all the time.' She choked back a sob.

'I'm so sorry.'

'I wanted to tell you over and over again but ...'

'It's simply too hard to put some things into words.' She decided to take a risk and told her friend what was going on with Lowena to show Polly wasn't the only one who'd kept things to herself.

'Well I never did. I bet she wanted to wring his neck. Kit was spot on calling him a bastard.'

'It's awful. I know Lowena's got her faults but don't we all? Her family is everything to her and doesn't deserve this.'

'You're right.' Polly's voice thickened. 'Some of us get exactly what we do deserve though and no one will ever convince me otherwise. Poor Jack's tried and failed all these years so don't you bother to start.'

An uncomfortable silence stretched between them.

'What I really came in to say is that Jack and me are moving on after the summer season finishes.' A glaze of tears clouded her eyes. 'It's time.'

'Move?' Nessa couldn't hide her dismay. 'Where?'

'We're still trying to decide.'

In other words they were arguing about it – something she'd never heard the couple do in all the time she'd known them. It struck her beyond awful that they survived losing their son only for grief and guilt to tear them apart now. Part of her wished Julian Bullen hadn't tracked them down but then she knew nothing of the pain and regret that must've been eating at her old friends for the last thirty years. 'But we're all working on the new course and other stuff. I can't do it all without you both!'

'I feel terrible letting you down … we both do but this should give you time to find someone else to take our places.'

Nessa pushed her coffee away. Polly and Jack's decision would force her to make hard choices. 'I'd better get on with cooking lunch because Kit will be in begging for food again soon.'

'Teenage boys have bottomless pits instead of stomachs.' Sadness suffused Polly's face. They both knew she'd be happy to cook all day for her own beloved son. 'I'd better be off.'

Once she left Nessa didn't try to hold back her tears.

'If you get lucky don't rush home on my account.' Ashley smoothed a tuft of hair that'd eluded his attempt to flatten it down.

'I doubt that'll happen with Lowena around.' He brandished the fancy bottle of wine he'd driven into Truro to buy. 'Think this will impress her?'

'Does that matter?'

Ward hesitated while he thought. 'Yeah, it does. It's not a deal breaker but family's important to both of us. Nessa's so nice it'll eat away at her if Lowena takes against me.' A wry smile slipped out. 'She hates me usin' the word nice because she says it makes her sound like a little girl who needs everyone to like her.'

'Hey what do I know about how to navigate a relationship? I'm not exactly an expert am I?'

Scratch the surface of Ashley's growing confidence and the uncertain woman underneath broke through again. 'Don't do this to yourself. Please.'

'Yes sir.' The playful salute didn't fool him. 'I'm gonna have a long soak in the bath and I'll see you when I see you.'

Ward heaved a sigh after she left the room. Nessa had enough on her plate without being burdened with his worries so he needed to snap out of it. The short walk worked its usual magic and cleared his head but as he strolled in through the gate a man's raised voice drifted out through Nessa's kitchen window.

'I can tell you now you're not getting your hands on half of my money. These days any judge worth their salt will tell you to stop doling out meals to old people and get a paid job. You can bloody well support yourself for a change instead of sponging off me.'

A red-faced, balding man stormed out of the house followed by Lowena hot on his heels.

'Go back to your precious Charlie,' she screeched.

The man jumped into a flashy black Porsche, sending gravel flying as he peeled out from the farm.

'Oh, it's you.' Ugly red blotches stained Lowena's face and neck as she spotted him. 'You'd better come in.'

He cautiously followed her into the kitchen and saw Nessa huddled over by the sink.

'I'm going up in my room,' Lowena snapped. 'Tell him what you like.' After she stalked out Nessa managed a weak smile.

'In case you didn't guess that was Antony. My brother-in-law.'

'Nice guy.'

'This is turning into a soap opera.' She glanced at the bottle he'd forgotten he was holding. 'Come on let's get out of here.'

'Your wish is my command.' Ward swept into his approximation of a princely bow. 'We need glasses and a corkscrew.'

'Or I could rip the cork out with my teeth and drink straight from the bottle.' A burst of harsh laughter broke out of her. 'But I suppose we'll be civilised.' She found the necessary items and shooed him towards the door. 'Take my mind off all this for heaven's sake.'

That he could do.

Chapter Nineteen

How she would've survived without Ward's support Nessa really didn't know. The initial one week's stay had turned into almost three but at least she and her sister were still on speaking terms. Barely. They stood together and waved as Lowena drove out of the farm with a sullen Kit slumped in the front passenger seat.

'They're not going far.' Ward squeezed her shoulder. 'Look at it this way. Tregereth House has its first guests. Unofficial ones anyway.'

'You might regret it.'

'Nah. I'm gonna put Kit to work starting to tame the gardens, and I can handle your sister.'

'Good luck with all that. At least she's calmed down a little. I haven't heard her baying for Antony's blood in a few days. I keep hoping they'll come to their senses and at least have an amicable divorce.' A slight frown wrinkled his forehead. 'You don't think so?'

'She's shrewd. Lulling him into a false sense of security. It's easy to recognise when you've been on the receiving end.'

'Sophia?'

'Yep. While we were working on what turned out to be our last album she was signing solo contracts left right and centre and cancelling shows, all behind my back.'

'That's terrible. Have you been writing more songs?' A flush of heat crept up his cheeks. 'Do I get to hear them?' Ward's hands tightened around her waist and he nuzzled soft tempting kisses on her neck.

'I could help fill your empty house tonight if you like?'

Despite the blatant attempt to avoid her question she couldn't help laughing. 'Is that the only reason you talked my sister into moving out?'

'Guilty as charged. I suppose I'd better ...' He hitched his thumb towards the road. 'It's kinda mean of me to leave Ash to deal with everythin'.'

'Come back later with your guitar and a toothbrush.' Nessa popped a kiss on his mouth. 'Off you go. I've tons of work to do and you've kidnapped my helper.'

'We can share Kit. Anyway what're you gonna do when he's back in school and the Greens leave? I know you're already missing Crispin's help.'

'I've no idea.' Worrying about how she'd cope kept her awake at night.

'I'll help you come up with something. I don't suppose you've heard anythin' from Crispin?'

'No.' A sigh slipped out. 'I wish he'd get in touch so I could at least pass on Aled Jones' message.'

'How are Polly and Jack doing?'

'Okay as far as I know.' A flash of sadness overtook her. 'Apart from day-to-day stuff we don't talk about anything that matters any longer.'

'Jack's roped me in a couple of times on his darts team at the pub when they've been short of folk but he's been quieter than the grave. Normally he's got plenty to say for himself when Polly's not around.'

A sudden brainwave struck Nessa. 'I could come up with something I need his help with. Maybe if I get him on his own I'll have better luck in persuading them to stay.'

'Yeah you might although I'm pretty sure I'll be the one

in luck tonight.' His raspy whisper hummed against her ear.

'You and me both.' She reluctantly stepped away. 'Off you go and keep the peace.'

Ward strolled in to the sight of Ashley and Lowena facing off in the kitchen.

'You're paying guests.' His sister's voice had an iron rod running through it. 'That means you don't wander in here and start cooking your own dinner.'

He spotted a trussed-up chicken ready for the oven and a pile of half-peeled potatoes on the cutting board.

'Your brother told me we were welcome to make this our home until I find something more permanent for me and Kit.' Lowena jabbed a finger in his direction. 'Ask him if you don't believe me.'

It would be a diplomatic miracle if he could appease both women. 'Lowena why don't you carry on with what you were in the middle of doing while I have a quick word with Ash?' His sister's mouth flapped open and shut like a fish but he steered her out into the hall.

'I thought I was in charge of dealing with the guests? Might've guessed you'd backtrack. It's what men do.'

Ward didn't attempt to defend his sex because she'd had her views coloured by ten years of marriage to a bully. 'This is different, Ash. You know what's goin' on and Kit's getting the rough end of all this. We don't have our business license yet so strictly speaking they can't pay us anyway and their rooms haven't been worked on yet so they aren't exactly palatial.' An idea struck him. 'She's an awesome cook and very organised. According to Nessa she runs just about every volunteer organisation around these parts. I bet she'd lap it up if you said you needed her help. I know we said we were goin' to wait on the kitchen renovation but if she helped you pull a plan together we might be able to get it done over the winter.' He pressed the point home. 'We've more rooms to paint. Furniture to buy. The electrician starts work next week and when he's done the plumber will be hot on his heels. Lowena's got good taste and I bet she'll know where to buy the kind of things this old place needs so rope her into helping you shop for furniture and stuff. It might help her see there's life after—'

'A bad marriage?' Her eyes narrowed. 'Good thing you're not as dumb as you look.' Ashley puffed out a sigh. 'Fine. I'll stick on my big girl panties and grovel to Miss Bossy. I'll consider it payback for all you've done helpin' me out.'

'Hey it works both ways, kid.' They didn't do emotional dumping and he didn't plan on starting now. 'I'm gonna get the grass cut then I'll be out for dinner.'

'And breakfast?'

'Maybe.' These days he didn't believe in tempting fate.

Nessa's heart thumped as footsteps crunched on the gravel. She smoothed down the deep rose silk dress and angled her legs the same way she'd seen Kate Middleton do. For some unfathomable reason she'd taken an inordinate length of time getting ready and the anticipation had kicked her nerves into high gear.

'I found your note although I'd have tracked you down

here anyway. It's your happy place.' Ward's honeyed drawl worked its usual magic.

'Let's not talk about family or problems tonight.'

'Whatever you want.'

'You. I want you.'

His slow grin evolved through the dusky night air. 'Snap.' The bench creaked as he sat next to her and Nessa's skin tingled as his gaze swept over her. 'You smell of hot, long summer days and the promise of even longer nights.' The huskiness thickening his voice was a huge turn-on. 'Is all this for me?'

'You mean the perfumed bath, face mask, make-up, plucking, shaving, high heels and new dress?' Obviously her attempt at casual sophistication failed because he was used to seeing her in sweaty work clothes with her hair scraped back in a rubber band. 'What is it they say? You can't turn a sow's ear into a silk purse?'

'That's not what I meant and you know it.' He made her skin thrum when he stroked her hands. 'I'm awed you consider I'm worth the effort. You're so beautiful tonight ... not that you aren't always but there's somethin' about you here ... now.'

Nessa found his awkwardness, the fumbled words and flushed face more intoxicating than any wine. She slid her fingers through his hair to drag him close. The first kiss was so feather light it could be mistaken for the breeze until he pulled a tiny moan from her throat and everything changed. After minutes or hours – she couldn't be sure which – he eased away and fixed her with glittering eyes.

'Should we take this inside?'

'Frightening guests out enjoying an evening stroll isn't

good for business.' Nessa exhaled a sigh. 'It stays light here far too long in the summer. Not good for secretive sex.'

'Secretive sex. I sure like the sound of that.' She loved his rumbling laughter. 'Tregereth has plenty of empty rooms to explore.'

'We'll have fun there another time but for now there's a chicken lasagne in my oven if you're interested?'

'It'll keep. Pasta makes a great midnight feast to keep the energy levels up.'

'I won't ask how you know.'

Shadows dimmed his smile. 'You can ask me any damn thing.'

'I was joking. Forget the rest of the nonsense.' They were old enough to know it would all still be there when the fun was over.

Chapter Twenty

'Just the man I need.' Nessa pounced on Jack. It'd taken several days and a lot of lurking around the farm to catch him on his own. 'I'm trying to decide on new bathroom fixtures for the guest rooms.'

'I thought you couldn't afford them yet?' His gaze turned wary. 'Not suddenly come into money have you?'

'No, but you won't be around when I'm ready to order. Unless your plans have changed?' Did she imagine the flicker of disquiet darkening his face? 'Come and look at some brochures with me.' Nessa chattered about paint colours and the merits of different showers until they reached the kitchen. 'Tea or coffee?'

'Nothing thanks.' He crossed his arms over his chest and fixed her with a firm stare. 'Say what you've got to say and I'll be on my way.'

She should've guessed he'd suss her out. 'Is it too much to ask for ten minutes after all these years?' Hopefully Ward was right about how best to play the situation.

'Play on his loyalty to your family and vice versa. Paint a grim picture of what it'll be like for them to start over somewhere else. Instead of the casual way they've been helping you offer them steady work so they don't have to look elsewhere. You could even think about bringing them in as partners down the line.'

He'd successfully tried something similar with Lowena so it might be worth a try. Her sister was lined up to be Tregereth House's official cook and deputy housekeeper when they opened for business and was working with him and Ashley now on the renovation.

'I'll have a coffee.' Jack dragged out a chair.

'With three sugars?' The corners of his mouth turned up. These days he only indulged his sugar addiction when he escaped his wife's eagle-eyes. A flush of tears blurred her gaze as it struck her how deeply she knew her old friends and Nessa swiftly turned away to fill up the kettle. If they were leaving because they genuinely wanted to she would still be upset but take it on the chin and move on. But this way? She'd fight until the little pink camper van drove out of the farm.

'Polly can't stay here. Not now you know about our Danny.' The crack in his voice tore at her.

'Why? Because she's convinced herself I think less of you both now? Surely you can't believe that? You're family. I love you both and that'll never change.' Tears leaked out of her eyes and trickled down her face.

'Oh lovey I've tried to talk her around but ...' He sounded helpless. 'It's tearing us apart and I don't know what to do.'

A burst of confidence filled her as she set a steaming mug down in front of him. 'Drink your coffee and listen to my idea. Well, it's Ward's actually but he's smart.'

'He's not a bad chap. For an American.' Jack's familiar smile creased his face. 'Out with it. How're we going to pull this off?'

The word "we" sent her spirits soaring.

'How's it going, Kit?' Ward stopped digging and tugged a large red and white spotted handkerchief from his pocket.

He whipped off his glasses and wiped the sweat from his face. 'You've only got a couple of weeks before school starts right?'

'I s'pose.' The boy didn't lift his head and continued to shovel fresh earth on the flowerbed. 'I'd rather stay here doing this.'

'It wouldn't be much fun in the middle of winter when it's cold and raining.'

'Don't care. I'm not going to be stuck in a bloody office wearing a suit the rest of my life like my dad.'

He needed to take care. Lowena would rightly string him up if he encouraged Kit to abandon his education. 'There are a lot of other options out there and a degree opens up all kinds of opportunities.'

'But I want to grow stuff like Aunt Nessa.' The pimples on his face stood out like angry red dots. 'What's wrong with that?'

'Nothing but—'

'I thought you'd understand but you're the same as the rest of them.' Kit's dismissive sneer cut through him. 'You chucked in your business degree for your music. What's the difference?'

He didn't ask where the boy found out all this, no doubt some came from trawling the internet but also people often overlooked quiet, surly teenagers and talked around and through them. 'I didn't chuck it in. I saw college through first and I'm usin' what I learned now.'

'You're telling me you'd rather run a lame bed and breakfast than this?' Kit shoved his mobile in Ward's face. The glamorous red-carpet picture of him and Sophia at

150

the Grammy awards ceremony in Los Angeles three years earlier sucked his breath away. 'You're full of shit.'

No one saw what lay behind those cheesy smiles. They'd just had a bitter argument in the limo about Sophia's increasing reliance on cocaine and heroin. She told him not to be a bore and laughed when he expressed his desire to return to their country roots instead of recording more crossover songs like the one nominated that night. Kit also didn't see Sophia six hours later with the medics working on her when she overdosed in the toilets at a post-awards party. The next day came their big split.

'Things aren't always what they seem, Kit. You've seen that with your folks.' Ward grasped his shoulder. 'I've started to get back into my music but I don't want all that crap again. It wasn't healthy.' He pointed to the photo. 'The heavy beard. Dark glasses. They can't cover up the fact I was pretty much a skeleton at that point and needed a spray tan to look half-human.' Kit flinched and he was afraid he'd gone too far but treating the young man as a child wouldn't drive the point home. 'Forget about me for a minute and focus on what *you* want. How about you research degree courses you might be interested in? Maybe something connected to the environment? It's never a bad idea to broaden your horizons.' Ward cracked a smile. 'After that if you still want to dig in the dirt in Cornwall you'll know the science behind it and do a better job. That make sense?'

'Dunno.' Kit kicked a rock away. 'Mum might listen but Dad? No way.' The boy gave him a long look. 'Got to choose haven't I? Keep quiet so they won't argue about me or tell them what I want and put up with the fallout.'

He restricted his reaction to a slight shrug.

'Thought so.' Kit's shoulders sagged then he straightened up and stuck the spade back in the earth. 'I'll get on the computer later.' The flicker of a smile returned. 'Next time I see Aunt Nessa I'll put in a good word for you.'

'Thanks pal. Now get back to work or I'll report you to the boss or should that be bosses?'

'Shit, tell me about it! Your bloody sister's almost worse than Mum.'

Ward shouldn't laugh and agree with the summing up but it was too tempting. Ashley and Lowena's mutual love of organisation and helping people meant they clicked in an uncanny way when it came to breathing life into Tregereth. He'd reached the point of following orders and signing off on their decisions with very little input needed from him. 'They're a formidable team.'

Kit rolled his eyes. 'I'd say—'

'Zip it,' he whispered urgently. 'We're bein' checked up on.' Ward lifted his hand. 'Hey, Ash, how's it goin'?'

'I'm fine.' Her gaze narrowed. 'What're you pair up to?'

'Deciding where to plant these new hydrangeas.'

'Yep, he thinks either side of the front door but I say the top of the drive is a better spot.'

Kit's swift response amused him. He played along and they bantered back and forth until Ashley's eyes started to glaze over.

'I'll leave you to it. The kettle's boiled when you're ready for coffee. Lowena's made a couple of different scones to try out. She's fine-tuning the menus.'

When she was out of sight they slapped high-fives in the air.

'You gotta be one step ahead kid.' Later Ward would kick himself for forgetting that.

Nessa hadn't seen anything wrong in googling Ward now that he'd told her about Sophia – professionally and personally. It might be a woman thing but she'd needed to see a picture of his ex-partner.

'Gettin' so used to me bein' around you didn't hear me come in?'

Before she could slam the laptop shut Ward's hand shot out to stop her.

'What's got you so engrossed?' The colour seeped from his face as he stared at the screen. 'I was goin' to tell you a few more details when I thought you wouldn't freak.'

'Really?'

'Yeah really.' Ward slumped on the chair next to her. 'It's not somethin' I brag about these days.'

'I'd no idea what a big deal "Spence + Sophia" were. All the awards and chart-topping songs. I know you told me she was beautiful but ... wow she makes me feel very ordinary.' She managed a self-deprecating laugh. 'Which of course I know I am.'

'You've no clue have you?' He caressed her cheek. 'I was a dumb guy who didn't see past Sophia's outward appearance until it was almost too late.' Ward picked up her hands. 'You've got more beauty and goodness in these than she had in her whole body. The rest of you is pretty damn fine too in my book.'

'You're trying to distract me.'

'Obviously unsuccessfully.' Sadness hummed through his thick drawl. 'I'll always deserve a measure of guilt over what happened to her in the end.'

'But you hadn't been together for ages when she died.'

'Doesn't matter.'

Nessa trailed her hand across his freshly shaven jaw. 'Was this all part of the reinvention?' The first picture of the couple startled her most because of the drastic change in Ward's appearance rather than his partner's breath-stopping beauty. The man she'd fallen in love with bore little resemblance to the skinny, bearded, unnaturally tanned, guitar-wielding singer with shoulder length black hair. 'You were terribly thin then.'

'Yeah,' he sighed, 'performing is tough on the body and Sophia hounded me all the time because she said our image was critical to our success.' A slight smile turned up the edges of his mouth. 'I've got Cornish pasties and butterscotch ice cream to thank for helping to reverse the trend.'

'And these?' Nessa touched his dark-framed glasses. 'I suppose contacts are more photogenic?' She whipped them off before he could answer and one quick look confirmed her suspicions. 'Plain glass. You don't need them do you?' For some reason that threw her off-kilter more than anything.

'I wanted to start fresh here so it made sense to have a new look … at least it seemed to then. I never meant to deceive you.'

'But you did.' Nessa pulled away. 'You've had plenty of chances to tell the truth. It might not seem a big deal to you but—'

'No, it is. I get that. You're wonderin' what else I've kept hidden.' He heaved a sigh. 'I could say there's nothin' important which is the God's honest truth but I'm pretty sure you won't believe me. Not yet anyway.' Ward dragged himself up to standing. 'I'll leave. Let you think things through. Give me a call when you're ready to talk.'

She longed to plead with him to stay but the words stuck in her throat. Over at the door he glanced back around and seemed on the verge of saying something before he shook his head and walked away.

Chapter Twenty-One

Ward hacked away at the brambles then tossed the brush cutter down in disgust. Every bloody thing reminded him of Nessa. It didn't help his temper to picture her sweaty and drop-dead gorgeous after working in the field at Pear Tree Farm. He'd endured a rollercoaster of emotions over the last five days since they parted on frosty terms and at the moment was plain angry with himself. He'd been stupid enough to confess his idiocy to Ashley in Lowena's hearing and the two women launched into him. They harped on about trust and honesty which was understandable considering what they'd both endured with their husbands but felt like a kick in the kidneys.

'Your sister said I'd find you out here.' Jack Green strode across the grass towards him. 'That's no way to treat your tools.' He tutted and picked up the sharp implement. 'Nessa thought you could do with hearing a bit of good news.'

Ward wiped his face with his arm. One upside to abandoning the fake glasses was not having to deal with them slipping and fogging up when he was working outside. 'You fancy a cold beer? I'll grab a couple of bottles and we'll sit on the patio.'

'Sounds good but don't tell Polly or she'll have my guts for garters. Drinking before lunch is a slippery slope according to her.'

'She's probably not talkin' to me anyway so you don't have to worry. I'm sure Nessa's been grumblin' to you both about my sordid past?'

'Maybe but she won't let it bother her. Not in the long run.'

'Then why hasn't she been in touch?' Ward's outburst made the other man jump. 'Sorry. It's not your fault. C'mon and I'll get those beers.' Luckily the kitchen was empty so he managed to sneak in and out again unobserved then re-joined Jack who'd dragged a couple of chairs under a shady tree.

'Bloody brilliant summer this.' Jack stretched out and took a long, noisy swallow from the ice-cold bottle. 'Good news is Polly and I are staying at the farm thanks to you.'

'That's awesome.'

'Polly's full of bright ideas. Too full probably so I hope Nessa doesn't regret the offer.' His smile faltered. 'I'm still working on convincing her to go back to Birmingham for a visit.'

'One thing at a time.' It hit him like a bash on the head from a blunt instrument that trying to rush things could be his problem too.

'I've been sent to ask if you'd like to come to ours for dinner tonight. Sort of a thank you.'

He dared not ask if they'd invited Nessa too.

'It'll be the four of us.' Jack's forthrightness made him smile. 'She grimaced when I told her but didn't say anything.'

'I'll take that.'

'Polly spends half her days now trying out new vegetarian recipes so goodness knows what we'll get fed.' Jack lumbered to his feet. 'I'd better be off. Between her and Nessa my to-do list is a mile long.'

'I'm the same. My two are hard taskmasters.'

'Seven o'clock.' Jack's face turned puce. 'Oh and one more message from the wife. She says wear the blue shirt and put on the sexy cologne. Her words not mine.'

'I sure hope so.'

'What're you two laughing at?' Lowena popped her head around the kitchen door. 'If you haven't got anything better to do than sit outside and drink in the middle of the day I'll find you something.'

'Yes ma'am.' Ward sprang to his feet while Jack made a quick escape. 'You're a wonderful woman and Tregereth is lucky to have you.' She threw him a suspicious look but his spirits were too high to be dented. Roll on seven o'clock.

No way would she be able to force down a single bite. It was a stupid idea and she should never have agreed but Polly resembled a whirlwind since she and Jack became official employees of Pear Tree Farm.

A serious talk. That's what she and Ward should have in private instead of enduring an awkward foursome. She'd thought a great deal over the last few days and was willing to concede she'd overreacted. Her sheltered upbringing hadn't offered many opportunities to go astray and Ward had made no attempt to make excuses for the bad decisions he made in the past.

Nessa fingered the rose silk dress and debated whether to change into something simpler. Secret, soft places tingled at the memory of his touch and she couldn't forget the searing glow in Ward's eyes the last time she wore it. An unwelcome blast of reality dumped a bucket of cold water on her dreams. He was probably tired of waiting for her to make the next move and only accepted Polly's dinner invitation out of politeness.

The grandfather clock in the hall struck seven. Too late to back out now. She grabbed her contribution to tonight's dinner – a bottle of Polly's new favourite rhubarb and strawberry gin – and left the house. Nessa hurried up the path but as it occurred to her she should probably slow down her left heel stuck in the ground and she went flying.

'No need to fall head over heels for me, sweetheart. I already fell hard for you so we're all good.' Ward's deep, rich voice hummed in her ear. Thankfully he'd clamped his strong arms around her waist and saved her from planting face first into the gravel. 'Aren't we?'

Nessa glanced up and met his worried expression. 'Yep.' She blinked away a rush of tears. 'I've been so stupid.'

'No, I'm the dumb one. Let me own this please.'

'Okay if you insist.' A weak giggle popped out and then they started kissing as if their lives depended on it.

'There you are!' Jack huffed down the path towards them. 'Polly was worried you pair were off arguing somewhere.' A broad grin spread over his face. 'I thought different.'

'Let's put her out of her misery.' Ward looped his arm through Nessa's. 'Got to keep this one safely on her feet.'

It was no hardship to snuggle against him and soak up a waft of the citrus cologne she loved.

'Hurry up you lot or my garden pea, mint and Cornish yarg soufflé will sink!' Polly waved frantically from the front step of the caravan.

'Oh no. World War Three is on us. A soggy soufflé,' Jack murmured under his breath then gave his wife a friendly wave. 'We're coming my love.' He hurried off but they didn't rush to join him and Ward turned back to her again.

'If it's okay with you we'll break loose as soon as we can?' He sounded unsure. 'The Tregereth mafia are lettin' me out for the night.' Tiny lines furrowed his brow. 'If I've got an invite that is.'

'You've got a standing one. Or whatever position we fancy.' Nessa blushed. She couldn't believe she said that.

'Naughty.' His eyes sparkled. 'Let's get dinner over with pronto.'

'I'm dishing up.' Polly almost dragged them inside. 'I changed my mind about eating outside because we'd get too many interruptions. I've put you two on the bench in by the window. It's a bit of a tight squeeze but you'll be alright if you don't mind being on top of each other.' She wagged her finger when they both sniggered. 'You've got dirty minds but I'm glad you've stopped being daft buggers. Hurry up and get settled as we've lots to talk about.'

Nessa resigned herself to a long wait before she could get her hands on Ward again.

'That was awesome.' Ward patted his stomach. 'I don't know how you pulled all that off in this tiny space. You've been hidin' your talents. Y'all are goin' to make a great team.'

'Thanks to you, mate,' Jack chimed in.

'Yes, it is thanks to him.' Nessa's adoring gaze made

him blush. 'It should've been staring me in the face to bring the two of you in properly before.'

The heat from Nessa's body pressed against his, seeped into his blood and drove him more than a little crazy as the conversation drifted into menu ideas for the garden-to-table courses.

'Don't know about you, Polly my love but I'm about knackered.' Jack's mouth stretched into a wide yawn. 'How about we let these young people go on home and we'll see to the dishes?' He shushed Ward before he could offer to help. 'There's not room in the kitchen for all of us and we've learned the knack of dodging around each other.'

Nessa squeezed his thigh under the table and gave him one of "those" looks. He wouldn't get a bird's eye view of the stockings he hoped were hidden under that slinky silk dress if he put a foot wrong now.

'Well okay and thanks again for a great evening.' He eased out from the narrow bench and hunched to avoid banging his head on the light when he stood up. 'Next time y'all will have to come to Tregereth and I'll get my new cook to whip us up somethin' good.'

'Lowena's working out well?' Polly said.

'She's smart, efficient and cooks like a dream. Ashley and I don't dare lift a finger in the kitchen and when we have guests they're gonna be well fed.' A wry grin sneaked out. 'Don't mind admittin' she still scares me some days.'

'Only some? She must be softening in her old age.' Nessa snickered.

'Softening? No way. C'mon let's get out from under these good people's feet.'

By the time they said their goodbyes and stepped outside he was grateful to take a few deep breaths. 'The air smells fresher tonight. Comin' in off the sea maybe?'

'Yes. They're all saying the heatwave's going to break any day now.' Nessa wiped a hand over her hot cheeks. 'Even I won't be sorry.'

They strolled down the path hand in hand and she didn't turn on any lights when they entered the house. With a secretive smile she locked the door behind them, led him into the kitchen and pulled down the blinds.

Ward yanked her to him, then peeled her out of the dress and hoicked her up on the table. 'Beautiful.' Nessa's soft blush deepened as he inched the stockings down her legs, tossed them aside and performed a similar vanishing act on her lacy white underwear. A flash of naughtiness lit up her eyes when he stripped off his own clothes in record time.

'What've you got in mind now?'

'My mind?' He chuckled. 'I'm afraid that doesn't have much to do with it sweetheart ... except for conjuring up the range of possibilities we can explore here.'

'Explore away.'

He didn't need to be told twice.

Chapter Twenty-Two

'Did you bring your guitar? You promised you would.'

Ward eased his long limbs into an expansive stretch, reminding her as she scootched over to the edge that she desperately needed a bigger bed. 'Yeah I drove down so the guitar is out in the car. Never used one during lovemaking before but I'm game to try anythin'.'

She prodded his solid chest, eliciting a playful ouch. 'You know *exactly* what I mean.'

'Do you realise it's only five a.m.?'

'Yes but I'm always up by six anyway. The campsite is full remember and it doesn't run itself and I've still a lot to do around the house.'

'Hey, stop and take a breath, honey. In fact take several long slow ones.' He reached for her hands. 'You've got Polly and Jack working alongside you now and I'm here.'

'But you've got Tregereth to see to.' Nessa twitched a smile. 'Unless you want Lowena and Ashley to take over?' She noticed his hesitation. 'Wow, that's your ultimate plan isn't it? Oh God you're not going back to Tennessee are you? I mean … I know your family are there and of course you will but … I'm rambling and being a mad woman aren't I?' Ward gathered her in his arms and hushed her.

'I'm kinda overwhelmed too if that helps? He brushed a lock of hair from her face. 'The last few months have been wild. Let's just hang in there together for now. We've made it to almost the end of August and your season will start to taper off in the next couple weeks. I am planning to go home sometime soon but not for good.' His forehead knitted in a deep frown. 'I sure hope you don't want me to?'

'No!'

'Pleased to hear it because I've got a half-renovated house, a long stay visa and my solicitor is wrapping up the business registration over the next few days. You and Cornwall are stuck with me. I never expected to fall in love with this place and you ... oh damn.' Ward scrambled up on his knees. 'I wanted to be more intentional the first time I said that to you.'

'If I say I love you too will that help?'

'Only if you mean it.' His voice turned to gravel.

'What do you think?'

'You need to hear somethin'.' Ward wriggled out of her grasp and yanked on his jeans and T-shirt. 'Don't go anywhere.' He thundered down the stairs, she heard him go out the front door – and then he was reappearing a couple of minutes later brandishing his guitar case.

Nessa didn't say a word as he settled cross-legged on the bed and started to tune the strings. The simple action transformed him and a sense of oneness with the instrument emerged as he coaxed it to life.

'I wrote this for you.' A dark flush heated his face. 'Us really.'

Halfway through the first verse her tears started. Other women might crave red roses and diamonds but this was far more precious. These were promises wrested from his heart. Love laid bare. Unadorned. As the last notes died away he set down the guitar and reached for her.

'The song says what I want to but find so damn hard without the props to hide behind.'

She caressed the early morning stubble roughening his cheek. 'I'm hardly the last word in eloquence. My parents were plain-spoken, ordinary people. They showed their love every day in the way they treated each other.'

'Mine are that way too.'

'Our sisters aren't flowery types either. It's funny how similar they are although they'd say we were crazy if we shared that insight with them.'

'Some things are best left unsaid'—Ward's mouth curved into a deeper smile—'at least if we want to live to see another day.' He cleared his throat. 'And I want a bunch of those with you.'

Nessa's heart thudded. 'Me too.'

Once before he made an utter fool of himself by assuming a woman felt a certain way but this time there was no guesswork needed. 'Did we just agree—?'

'Yes. Not yet but soon'—Nessa leaned in to kiss him—'and we keep this to ourselves. I can already hear Lowena chastising me.'

'Yeah Ashley will too.' He'd learned pragmatism the hard way. 'How're we goin' to celebrate?'

'Take a wild guess.' She tugged him down on top of her.

By the time they were both breathless and bathed in sweat the sun was blazing in through the open window.

'Nessa, are you alive in there? Why aren't you answering your mobile?' Lowena's sharp voice drifted up. 'Is Ward still there?'

'Reality strikes again. I won't be long.' With a sigh she pushed him away and swung her legs out over the bed. 'I'll be down in a minute,' she yelled towards the window.

Ward stretched back out and watched her tug on a pair of cut-off denim shorts and a baggy grey T-shirt before she hurried out of the room. Lowena's voice carried and he picked up snippets of a muttered conversation and a mention of his name. Nessa reappeared but minus her sunny smile. 'What's wrong?'

'You need to get back to Tregereth right now. Ashley's husband turned up.'

All the happiness sucked from the room. 'Shit.' While she carried on talking he dragged his clothes back on and grabbed his wallet and keys off the dresser. All that sunk in through his panicked fog was Bunny Radnor landing on the doorstep first thing and forcing his way into the house. 'I should've known. Dammit. Is Ashley okay?'

'She was when Lowena left. This isn't your fault.' She touched his arm. 'Let's go see what we can do to help.'

'But you've got work to do here.'

Nessa's face softened. 'We're a team. Remember? You're there for me and I'm there for you.'

Ward wasn't stupid enough to protest that he could handle it. 'Do you want to let Polly and Jack know where we've gone?'

'Yes, I should.' She shooed him away. 'You go on and I'll get a lift with Lowena.'

'Are you sure?'

'Ashley needs you. We'll only be a few minutes behind.' She pressed a kiss on his mouth. 'Don't do anything stupid before I get there.'

'Afterward is okay?' The half-hearted joke made her smile. 'I'm off.' He was glad he'd brought the car so he wouldn't arrive out of breath after running all the way to

Tregereth. If Bunny laid a finger on his sister he'd make him pay.

Nessa's stomach churned as they drove out of the farm. Her sister wasn't easily rattled but Ashley's husband obviously unnerved her. 'Tell me some more. What's the full story?'

Lowena's white hands gripped the steering wheel. 'I was doing a practise run on breakfast to get my timings right for when our first guests arrive – I know next Easter is a long way off but it doesn't hurt to be prepared – and someone started to ring the doorbell. They wouldn't stop so I went out to give whoever it was a piece of my mind. I recognised him immediately from pictures I'd seen.' She shuddered. 'His language was vile. He's a complete pig. He pushed in past me yelling for Ashley and found her in the kitchen.' Her voice quavered. 'I felt awful running out to get help but I thought it best.'

'I think you were smart. Should we call the police?'

'Not yet. Hopefully Ward can calm down the situation.'

Nessa wouldn't bet on it by the thunderous expression on his face when he flew out of the farm. She clutched the edge of the seat as Lowena jerked the wheel and turned into Tregereth. With none of her usual care her sister abandoned the car outside the front door and they ran into the hall. She expected to hear a loud argument going on but the absence of any sound was unnerving.

A sudden loud, desperate wail shattered the silence.

'Oh my God he's dead. You've killed him!' Ashley's shrill voice turned Nessa's stomach and she took off running. A massive wave of relief swept through her when she burst through the kitchen door and saw Ward standing there – white as a ghost but apparently unharmed. That dissipated quicker than snow in the sun when she spotted a man slumped on the floor with his back against the cast-iron range. A sickening trickle of blood dripped down from his matted blond hair.

'I had to stop him Nessa. He tried to kill her.' Ward's gruff voice cracked and he broke into loud, hitching sobs when she wrapped her arms around his neck.

'No one's going to blame you.' If she was wrong what would happen to them?

Chapter Twenty-Three

Ward was vaguely aware of Lowena bustling past them and held his breath as she crouched down to press her fingers against Bunny's neck.

'He's alive. Ring 999 now.'

He sagged in Nessa's arms. 'I didn't mean ... look at Ash's neck. I couldn't ...' The horror replayed in his head. Radnor's foul tirade echoing through the house. His race to the kitchen. The terrifying sight of Ashley pinned to the wall with her husband's hands around her throat. He'd launched himself at his brother-in-law's back and dragged him off. The glorious sound of her gulping breaths reassured him she was okay but the brief moment of satisfaction coincided with the sound of Bunny's head smacking against the range.

'Y'all know we can't put off calling the police any longer.' Ashley's sober words sunk in.

'You're not callin' any damn police.' Bunny groaned and struggled to sit up. 'You're a brainless moron. God knows why I married you. You're not even good in bed. It's like screwin' a dead fish. I slipped and banged my head. End of story. Right?'

'You tried to kill my sister. I'm not lettin' you get away with that!' Ward's voice soared.

'You're as stupid as she is. Do you want to rot in prison while the police make up their minds whose story to believe?'

He hated to see Bunny's point. They were foreigners with no knowledge of the British justice system. Even with Ashley's testimony who knew what might happen?

'Oh no you can both forget that. I'm not perjuring myself.' Lowena's steely tones matched her ramrod posture. She'd already made the emergency call while they were talking.

'Please do it for me.' Nessa's quiet plea took him by surprise but then she slapped her hand over her mouth and stared in horror at Ashley. 'Oh God I'm so sorry I shouldn't assume that's what you want.'

'What she wants?' Bunny gingerly touched the back of his head and grimaced at the smears of blood on his fingers. 'What right's she got to—?'

'Every bloody right!' Ward got in his brother-in-law's face. 'You've made her life a misery for ten years and when she tried to leave you hounded her down.' He grabbed a handful of Radnor's shirt. 'Look at her. See what you've done.'

'Yeah, yeah I'm sorry. All right?' Bunny grouched.

'Sorry? You think that's enough?'

Lowena tapped his shoulder. 'If it's Ashley's wish and we're going to pull off this ridiculous travesty you need to back off. The medics will be here any minute and they're not going to be fooled if we're at each other's throats.'

'You'll go along with it?' Nessa's breath caught in a sob.

'When have I not been on your side? I'll probably regret it but—'

'It's still your choice, Ash,' Ward said quietly. Indecision fluttered across her pale features. 'Say the word and we'll call the police. Whatever the fallout is we'll deal with it.'

'Leave it alone. All I want is him out of my life. A divorce.'

'You got a problem with that?' he snarled at Bunny.

'Nah, I'll be glad to be rid of her.'

He turned back to his sister. 'Do you want them to take a look at your neck?' Livid red finger marks were blossoming around her throat.

'No. I'll go and wrap a scarf around them. They'll fade in a few days. They did before.'

'*Before?*' An angry cloud blurred his vision. 'You said he never—'

'Sorry. I lied.'

There wasn't time to argue because the wailing sirens were getting closer.

'I suggest we all try to look a great deal more concerned about this … creature.' Lowena glared at Bunny. 'If no one objects I'll offer to follow them to the hospital in my car. I'm the least likely to contradict his story.'

The next few minutes were a whirlwind as the paramedics arrived, did their work and removed Bunny on a stretcher. An uncomfortable silence fell around the three of them as Lowena closed the front door on her way out. Ward couldn't drag his eyes away from the bloodstains on the floor. He'd come close to killing a man which wiped out every preconceived idea of who he was and what he was capable of. But today wasn't the first time Bunny hurt his sister and would've undoubtedly done so again.

'We'd all do everything we could to protect those we love. You're no different.' Nessa attempted to reassure him.

'If you beat yourself up over this you'll have me to reckon with.' Ashley planted herself in front of him. 'You saved my life and if they try to lock you up they'll need to do the same with me because I'll fight them tooth and nail.'

He dropped it. They knew this would haunt him for years to come but at the end of the day he'd done what was necessary to keep his sister safe. 'How about we clean up and have some British medicine?' The question earned him puzzled looks. 'Tea. Isn't it the cure for everything?'

'I could do with a stiff drink and I don't mean strong PG Tips either.' His sister shuddered. 'Lowena keeps tryin' to pour that godawful stuff down me.'

He fetched a bottle of whisky and three glasses. Ward poured them all generous measures and raised his glass. 'To peaceful Cornwall!'

Nessa wasn't keen on whisky and only took a few sips before setting aside her glass. She glanced down over herself in dismay. Braless under her old T-shirt. Uncombed hair. Heaven alone knew what her face looked like. At a guess there were smears of last night's make-up and a noticeable amount of stubble rash. 'I think I need a shower and some clean clothes before I do anything else.'

Ward's colour rose. 'Yeah. Me too.'

'I've gotta say you do both look a little rough around the edges.' Ashley smirked. 'I appreciate you didn't stop to worry what you looked like though before comin' to my rescue.'

'Anythin' for you, sis.' Ward squeezed her shoulder. 'We don't care what folks think do we, Nessa?'

'We certainly don't.' A torrent of joy rushed through Nessa as she locked eyes with him.

'OMG.' Ashley stared at them in horror. 'Don't tell me you two are … you haven't asked her to—?'

'No.'

She found Ward's clipped response amusing. It was ninety percent true because he hadn't proposed in so many words.

'Don't take this personally Nessa but he made a huge mistake with that cow Sophia.'

'I know. He's told me all about her. I love your brother very much,' Nessa said calmly. 'We're working things out at our own pace.'

'Wow, you're not as sweet as you look are you?' Ashley grinned.

'I'll take that as a compliment.'

'We'll take this as your official warning.' Ward linked hands with Nessa. 'Don't add anythin' else or we'll likely fall out.'

'I reckon you might be the perfect pair. Now I'll get things cleared up here and he can take you home.'

'Are you sure?'

'Absolutely. Shoo.'

'Oh.' Nessa's phone dinged with an incoming text. 'It's Lowena.' Her heart thudded as she skimmed through the message. 'Bunny is doing okay. They've given him a few stitches and are keeping him in overnight for observation in case of a concussion. No one questioned his explanation for the "accident" and my awesome sister backed him up.'

'We owe her big time.' Ashley's voice trembled.

'Don't worry she'll never let us forget it.' The injection of humour gave everyone permission to smile. 'Now some of us have a business to run.' She squeezed Ward's hand. 'If you don't mind being my taxi service you can drop me off at the farm then come back here.'

'Happy to help but ... I'm banished?'

'You've got work to do.'

'He sure does.' Ashley wagged her finger.

'Fine. Gang up on me you evil women.'

An unfamiliar sound made them all turn and stare out of the window. 'Yes! Finally.' The gentle patter of rain on the glass increased until it settled in a persistent rhythm. 'My plants will be so happy. I've been watering them but they could do with a good soaking.' She grinned at Ashley. 'Here's the proper Cornish summer weather you keep hearing about.'

Ward grabbed her hand. 'C'mon. We're a mess anyway so let's make the most of it.' He almost dragged her through the house and out the front door. Within minutes they were soaked to the skin but couldn't stop laughing and kissing. 'It's a great excuse for a hot shower when we reach your place.'

'I might've guessed you have an ulterior motive.' She wiped at the rain blurring her eyes although they could be tears of happiness. Nessa couldn't be sure and didn't really care.

'Always.'

'We'll get your car soggy.'

'Do I look like a guy who cares?' He drew her into another kiss. 'I'm takin' it back as soon as we find one for me to buy.'

'We? I won't be any use. I've never bought a car in my life. I'm still driving my dad's old Ford Fiesta.'

'I've bought plenty of vehicles in the States but I want to choose somethin' you're happy with too.'

Nessa didn't need the "why" spelled out. Not today.

Chapter Twenty-Four

Ward leaned against the doorframe watching the sun rise. Taking stock. He could hardly believe it was almost the middle of September already. He'd barely stopped working for the last couple of weeks and was pretty sure he'd grown a paintbrush as a third hand. But even he could start to envision what Tregereth would look like in a few months. The rewiring was complete and the plumber had done as much as he could until the new bathroom fittings arrived. They'd agreed on the kitchen plan Lowena put together and ordered all of the new appliances, granite countertops and plain Shaker style cabinets. Ashley and Lowena kept disappearing at regular intervals and coming back loaded down with everything they could fit into Lowena's car from small furniture, paintings and lamps to yesterday's apparently unmissable bargain of a massive chandelier for the dining room. The thing looked in poor shape to him but Lowena swore she could restore it over the winter and he didn't doubt that for a moment.

The schools were generally back in session which meant Nessa's visitor numbers had eased off so today he had special plans with her. She balked at first because her first garden-to-table course started next week but he'd roped in Polly and Jack so between the three of them they talked her into taking the day off. He smiled as Ashley's tuneless singing drifted out from the kitchen. Last night's email from her attorney confirmed that Bunny had been served with the legal papers and had promised not to contest her application for a no-fault divorce. There were plenty of faults she could drag up but she'd chosen to draw a line under her intolerable marriage and Ward couldn't blame her.

'Are you seriously takin' Nessa to that mine today? That's not very romantic.'

Ward glanced up when his sister arrived to join him but didn't rise to her prodding. 'Haven't you got anythin' better to do than hassle me? If Lowena catches you slackin' off she'll—'

'I can't wait to hear my intentions. Do illuminate me.'

He was surprised to see Nessa's sister materialise out of thin air. 'Oh hi, I thought it was your day off?'

'Fridays usually are but I'm taking next Monday instead because I have an appointment with my solicitor.' Her expression turned stony. 'I'm starting divorce proceedings.'

If Ward admitted how much he admired her she'd scoff and order him not to be such a touchy-feely American. Her close friendship with Ashley still surprised him but they had enough in common to make their differences irrelevant. They'd slipped into working together seamlessly and he'd no doubt that when they opened, Tregereth would run like a well-oiled machine. After the two women convinced him to take the plunge he'd agreed with George Yeatman to have the attic reconfigured over the winter into an upmarket suite to appeal to people who wanted a more luxurious experience.

'How's Kit getting on back at school? He never says much when I ask him.'

'Really good.' Lowena tweaked a smile. 'He's only got to survive this year. It's lucky we didn't have to move out of the area so he could stay on at Truro College. The Horticulture and Landscape Design course at the Eden Project he plans to do should suit him down to the ground. Pun intended.' She smiled at her own joke. 'That's all thanks to you.'

'If I was out of line encouraging him I'm sorry.'

'Oh I didn't mean that, you silly man. I'm still cross at myself for being so wrapped up in my own problems I didn't see how miserable Kit was.' She tutted. 'Even Antony grudgingly admitted his share of the blame the other day. That was a first.'

It must be the only thing her stubborn husband had given way on but Ward kept that thought to himself.

'Antony can't complain too much because Kit will have a degree at the end of it even if he won't be an accountant or qualified for one of the other professions his father considers suitable.' Lowena brushed her hands together. 'I've got work to do even if you don't.'

He couldn't help smiling as she strode off in her usual determined manner.

'She sure is a force of nature.' Ashley's wry observance was spot on. 'The woman's right though so I'm off too.'

In the distance the church clock struck seven and he drank his last slug of coffee before wandering back inside the house. He wasn't picking Nessa up until mid-morning so would tackle some of the jobs on his endless to-do list now. He'd settled in his mind how to play things with her today and hoped he could pull it off.

Nessa's heart lifted at the beep-beep of Ward's horn. It would sound silly to admit she'd miss his rented blue Kia but it seemed a part of him now or rather part of their story. Watching him clamber out – an action requiring some amount of bending and stooping on his part – she thought how much healthier he looked. His hair had grown out into a sexy, tousled style, his sparkling eyes were more visible without the abandoned glasses and she never saw him wearing the old dark, baggy clothes these days.

She'd startled awake in the middle of the night fretting about the surprise he'd promised her today. Nessa was pretty sure it wouldn't be a proposal and couldn't decide if that pleased or disappointed her. The sun had returned this morning but without the intensity of the last few months. He'd asked her to wear hiking boots but bring a pair of sandals to change into. Hopefully her new dark jeans, sapphire blue T-shirt and white cotton jumper would be appropriate for whatever he had in mind.

'You smell wonderful but then you always do.' He swept her into a hug and kissed her until she could barely breathe. 'You'll tempt me to stay here and whisk you off upstairs if I'm not careful but then we'd miss out.'

'On what?' Nessa knew he wouldn't answer but couldn't resist asking.

'You'll find out.' He checked his watch. 'The traffic should be light but we'll go ahead and leave. It'll give us plenty of time to take our walk first.'

Nessa obediently jumped in and sat back to enjoy the drive. For all she knew it could be five minutes away or five hours. Polly and Jack were safely in charge so she didn't have to rush back for anything. They headed west and the scenery lost the softness of the Polgarth Valley becoming more rugged and harsh the closer they got to Redruth. Somehow it didn't surprise her when he turned off at the signpost for the Poldark Mine. 'We're going underground? If you'd said I would've brought a jacket.'

His smile deepened. 'We're just goin' to park there for now but we can do the tour another day if you'd like. If you're up for it I'd enjoy a hike across the cliffs to see where Wheal Rosen used to be. It's about a mile each way and we're not in a rush as long as we're back here by noon.'

What happened at noon was another mystery. 'It's fine with me. It's a lovely day and I enjoy getting out more now it's quieter.' Nessa's lingering anxieties floated away on the breeze and drifted out across the sparkling blue sea. They strolled along the narrow path brightened by colourful fragrant wildflowers that clung to the rough ground.

'I'm going to book my trip back to Tennessee soon so I'm afraid you'll have to do without me for a couple of weeks early next month … unless I can persuade you to come too?'

A sigh slipped out before she could stop it. 'Oh, I'd love to but—'

'It was worth a try.' He brushed off her attempt to apologise. 'Don't worry we'll go together when things are quieter at the farm. I reckon Polly and Jack might be able to cope for a few weeks in the New Year?'

'I don't see why not.' Nessa couldn't help smiling. 'That would be awesome. I don't start my garden-to-table courses again until the spring so the timing's perfect.'

'Yeah I think so too.' He stopped walking and wrapped

his arms around her. 'I've got financial stuff to see to and I need to see my folks. They deserve to hear about everythin' that's gone on straight from the horse's mouth.'

'I don't see any tail.' She patted his backside.

Ward rolled his eyes at her. 'I promise I'll be back before the pears are ready to pick.'

She managed to nod through the tears stinging her eyes. 'We'd better keep going or we'll be late for whatever it is we might be late for.' The sly comment made him laugh.

'There it is.' Ward pointed to the dilapidated remains of an old engine house a few hundred metres away. 'That pile of bricks is all that's left of Wheal Rosen. It was one of the first to close back in the day because it didn't have the financial backing of the larger mines.' He let go of her hand to scramble over the uneven ground and when Nessa caught up she discovered him crouched down with his hand pressed into the ground. The only sounds came from the herring gulls swooping and squawking overhead and the sea brushing against the cliffs before swooshing back out again. As he straightened up and turned around his eyes were suspiciously bright.

'Ready?'

She grasped his outstretched hand and they didn't talk much on the walk back. 'What now?'

'Lunch.' Judging by her frown his casual reply puzzled her. Did Nessa have the wrong impression about today? Would she be disappointed that the surprise wasn't a diamond ring? He'd assumed they were on the same page as far as not rushing into anything. 'The café serves great

pasties although I'm sure they're not as good as yours.'
He put on a sad face. 'I thought all Cornishwomen made
them for the men they love?'

Her cheeks turned pink. 'If you can resist eating one
now I'll make us a couple tonight.' She prodded his firm
stomach. 'Pasty gut is a real thing you know. Look at
George Yeatman if you need proof.'

'I'll order a salad to make you happy in fact I'll do
anythin' to make you happy.' She looked as surprised as
he felt when that popped out. 'Uh we'd better go in or
we'll be too late.'

'Why're you in such a rush? Surely they don't stop
serving lunch anytime soon?'

Never again would he keep secrets from Nessa. She was
far too sharp and persistent. Ward steered her towards the
café but as soon as they stepped inside a burly man with a
thick ginger beard accosted them.

'There you are. We were afraid you weren't coming.
Who's this pretty maid? Your fan club?' His warm
chuckling laugh reverberated around the small space.

'Nessa Vivian, my … girlfriend.' If she'd been curious
before she was totally bewildered now. Ward caved in.
'This is Red Nancarrow. He sings with The Wheal Boys
who specialise in old Cornish mining songs.'

'And new ones when we get the chance.' Red winked.
'Don't we, boy?'

'You sure do. Are you on soon?'

'Five minutes. Get yourself a drink and find a seat.
We've got a good turnout today.' He slapped Ward's
shoulder. 'We'll catch up with you after.'

'Aren't you a dark horse?' A smile played around

Nessa's lips. 'Let's do what the man says. I've no intention of missing this.'

His stomach clenched as they walked into the crowded café.

'Sit down before you pass out.' Nessa pushed him towards a chair. 'It'll be awesome. I can't believe you did all this behind my back.'

'Sorry. I wanted to tell you … well I did and I didn't. Ash doesn't know either if that makes it any better.' Ward dipped his head. 'Don't suppose it does.' He took her warm smile as a sign he'd been forgiven. 'I tracked them down online and we got together the other day.'

A ruddy-faced woman bustled onto the tiny stage. 'I know they don't need introducing to most of you so I'll let The Wheal Boys speak for themselves or rather sing!'

The first few songs were old favourites and he noticed most of the crowd joining in with the choruses. When Red asked for a bit of quiet he tightened his grasp on Nessa's hand.

'We've a rare old treat for you today. A song written by our new mate Ward Spencer.' The singer jabbed a finger in his direction. 'He's American but we won't hold that against him because he's got Cornish blood running through his veins.'

Everyone stared at him while they listened to the brief rundown on Bill Tremayne's life and Ward's storied musical career.

'If you aren't wiping away a tear by the end of this there's something wrong with 'ee.' Red wagged a warning finger in the air.

A hush fell on the room as the music started and

Ward tucked this moment away with his other treasured memories. The first day he heard one of his songs on the radio. His first performance at the Grand Old Opry. The first gold record.

The last notes faded away into the sort of silence all artists craved and dreaded in equal measure. For several heart-thumping seconds it was always impossible to tell if it was a good or bad omen. The fifty or so people crammed into the small space burst into enthusiastic applause and Ward allowed himself to breathe again. Music was a crucial part of who he was and it'd been foolish to think he could push it away like a neglected guitar to the back of the wardrobe.

'That was incredible.' Tears trickled down Nessa's face.

He recognised a tinge of sadness mixed in with her obvious pride and wondered how he could reassure her this wasn't a threat to them and their future together. Ward hoped he could find the words to tell her what she needed to hear.

Chapter Twenty-Five

The unease pitted in the base of her stomach grew as she watched Ward smiling and accepting everyone's congratulations. Nessa kept hoping he'd make his excuses so they could leave but that didn't happen until The Wheal Boys packed up their van and set off for another gig. On the drive home there might as well have been a Perspex shield between them. They talked – if it could be called talking – but only about extraneous stuff like the welcome change in the weather.

'I need to buy the beef for our pasties. If you want to pop back to Tregereth you can drop me in the village and I'll walk back to the farm after I've done my shopping.'

'Sweetheart, forget the pasties. We need to talk.' He rested a hand on her knee. 'I reckon our spot in the orchard will do us fine.'

Our spot. Nessa loved the sound of that but still couldn't shake the picture of his brilliant smile and undeniable happiness surrounded by people who appreciated his music. If he chose a life with her she'd be denying him that, at least at the level he deserved. He wouldn't remain satisfied with the adulation of a small gathering in a Cornish café.

'Don't assume anythin'. You know what that does – makes an ass of you and me.'

She struggled to smile but jerked her head away to stare out of the window so he couldn't see the tears blurring her vision. By the time they arrived back at the farm she'd resigned herself to the inevitable. 'I need to pop up and see Polly first to make sure she hasn't had any problems while I've been out.' Nessa leapt from the car when he parked and raced off before he could stop her or offer to come along too. She banged on the caravan door and threw it open as Jack yelled out for her to come in.

'Is Polly here?'

He chuckled. 'Have you forgotten it's Friday afternoon? You should know her routine after all these years. She had her hair appointment at two o'clock and then went for tea and a gossip with Dorrie Biscombe.' Jack's gaze narrowed on her. 'Is everything all right? Did you have a good day out?'

Nessa slumped down on the sofa beside him and launched into a stumbling, tearful ramble about how much she loved Ward but that things could never work between them. Jack looked bemused as she tried to explain what happened at lunchtime.

'I'll put the kettle on.' He patted her arm. 'Ward's a good chap. You've got to have a little faith. He won't let you down.' Jack disappeared into the neat galley kitchen and soon returned with their tea. 'Here you go.' The fact he made hers in one of the fragile pink flowered cup and saucers Polly saved for special occasions set her tears off again. 'I think it's a chocolate biscuit day.' Nessa sniffed, wiped her nose and meekly took one from the tin he'd set down on the table. 'Now why don't you try again and tell me what's got you so rattled?'

Her old friend possessed the same quality as Ward when it came to listening and gave himself quietly and whole-heartedly. By the time she finished a large chunk of her anxiety had seeped away. 'Aren't you going to tell me I'm being silly?'

'No because it's not an unreasonable conclusion you came to.' He crunched on a biscuit. 'But don't you think the poor chap deserves the benefit of the doubt?'

'I suppose.'

'Off you go and put him out of his misery.' He patted her hand. 'Don't forget what his so-called successful lifestyle did to him. I'd bet everything I've got he's no desire to go down that road again.'

'Whatever would I have done if you and Polly left?'

'Rubbed along all right. Most people do.' His eyes clouded. 'It's either that or fall apart.'

'I can't imagine how you—'

'No and I hope you never do.' His gentle, firm tone made it clear the conversation wasn't going in that direction.

Nessa threw her arms around him. 'You're the best and Polly's a lucky woman.'

'Am I indeed?' Her smiling friend poked her head in the door. 'What's he done to deserve a beautiful young woman throwing herself at him or don't I want to know?' Her husky laughter filled the caravan.

'You'll have to ask him. I can't keep Ward waiting any longer. Love the hair by the way.' This week it resembled a bright yellow cactus perched on top of her head. Nessa breezed out past her and took off at a run.

'I could do with some company.' Ward's familiar rich drawl stopped her half way down the path. He stood in front of the entrance to the walled garden and there were deep frown lines etched into his lean face. She'd ruined this special day for him but maybe it could be salvaged if she seized this second chance.

He surreptitiously crossed his fingers. Maybe Nessa's heightened colour and obvious nerves were a good sign.

'Jack has knocked some sense into me.'

'Good to hear.' He'd buy his friend a whole crate of real ale for this. 'You wanna show me how your pears are comin' along?'

'No man has ever asked me that before … at least not without a suggestive wink.'

'I can do one of those if you like.' He followed through and loved it when she couldn't help giggling.

By unspoken agreement they strolled in together and talked about nothing more serious than how to get rid of the bugs eating her cabbages and whether she should plant more runner beans next year.

'Those aren't ripe yet.' She stopped by the pear trees. 'They're almost ready though for poaching, pickling and jam making and I'll start on that next week. I used to help my mum and it's still one of my favourite things to do.' Nessa cleared her throat. 'If you want to eat one ripe off the tree you'll need to be back by about the third week of October.'

'That'll work.' The promise made her face heat up. Ward nodded towards the bench. 'I reckon your mom's favourite spot is perfect for our chat.'

'She'd like that … and you.'

'You think so?'

'I know so.'

They sat together and with her head nestled into his

shoulder the peace of the late afternoon settled around them.

'Let me say one thing, then I promise to listen. Properly this time.'

He couldn't help smiling when she told him everything Jack said. 'Yeah, he nailed it. Did it make me happy when people liked my song today? Course it did. I'm human, Nessa and an artist at my core.' He shrugged. 'We need feedback from other folk but you've gotta believe me when I say that's enough. I'm done with chasing the next hit record and all the crap that comes with it. I'd rather chase a beautiful, opinionated Cornishwoman with green fingers and awesome legs.' He choked on a laugh. 'I'm tryin' to be romantic but it never works unless I'm writing song lyrics.'

Nessa's eyes shone. 'I've never been much for flowery stuff.' A giggle bubbled out of her. 'Unless it's to do with growing them and I'm pretty good at that.

'You sure are. You're good at a whole bunch of things. Do you think when your pears are ready for eatin' we might be ready for ...' Every last one of the rational, sensible things he'd planned to say flew out the window. 'Heck you know I love you and want a life with you and I'm pretty damn sure you feel the same. I was gonna wait—'

'Don't.'

'Don't?' He felt the blood seep from his face and guessed it was as white as the climbing rose shedding petals on the ground by his feet.

'Don't wait.' Nessa's breathy plea burst through the panicked fog clouding his brain. 'The answer is yes.'

'Did you just agree to marry me?'

'Yes.' Her expression darkened. 'Unless that wasn't the question in which case I might have to rethink my answer?'

'No! I mean yes it was the question and don't you dare change your mind.' His vehemence made her roar with uninhibited laughter. All he could think was how lucky he was. 'A lot of folk will say we're out of our minds.'

'Will that bother you?'

'Sure won't but I'm not havin' anyone spoilin' it for you.'

'You really think they could?' She stroked his face. 'Let's keep it as our secret until you come back. I wish I could join you but … I don't want you to think for one minute that we're less important than—'

He silenced her with a lingering kiss and didn't ease away until he calculated he'd done a thorough enough job. 'Hey I totally agree you need to concentrate on doin' a good job with your first garden-to-table courses so you can build on that next spring. One reason I fell in love with you is your passion for making a success of something that was important to your family. My family are everything to me too.' His mood darkened as unsettling memories flooded back. 'I forgot that for a while when being "famous" mattered more and I paid a hefty price. Poor Ashley did too because I took my eye off the ball where she and her lousy marriage were concerned.'

'Don't beat yourself up. You aren't the only person in her life. Your parents. Her friends. Co-workers. Other people must have known too or at least guessed something wasn't quite right and did nothing. I've been no better with Lowena.' She sounded sad. 'She mastered the stiff upper lip thing so well and I didn't push her on it. Sometimes there's only so much we can do for another person. They've got to come to their own conclusions and make their own choices. No more negativity tonight.' A wicked twinkle sneaked back into her eyes. 'Did I mention I got a new king-sized bed delivered yesterday?'

'You know you didn't.' He tightened his arms around her. 'Does it need testin' out?'

'Are you offering?'

'I sure am.' Ward nuzzled kisses down her neck, lingering at the hollow at the base of her throat. 'Secret engagements deserve even more of a celebration because there's no ring to show off.'

'I love your thought process.'

She almost dragged him to his feet and they made a quick dash for the house, laughing and stumbling up the stairs in their haste.

'Yeah, I like it.' The simple oak-framed bed took up most of the room and he bent down to prod the mattress. 'So far so good but you know what they say don't you?' She raised an eyebrow. 'The proof of the pudding is in the eating.' Ward pushed her down on the bed and knelt over her. He bounced up and down. 'Yep. Decent springs. We should be good.'

'Prove it.'

'Happy to oblige.'

They both ditched their clothes in record time and he caught Nessa's heightened colour as her gaze travelled over him. 'What were the chances in this big 'ole world that we'd find each other?'

'That's very profound and I've absolutely no idea but who cares? Come here and love me.'

That was all the encouragement he needed.

Chapter Twenty-Six

How could days both drag and fly by simultaneously? Nessa had asked herself that question for every one of the last fifteen evenings in a row since Ward left at the beginning of October, when she reluctantly fell into bed alone. She smoothed out the new duvet cover she bought last week, the deep burgundy and cream broad stripe suited the room but shouldn't look too feminine when her lover returned in six days.

'It's only me.' Polly's cheerful voice drifted up. 'I'm back from having my hair done and I've got news.'

'Something good I hope?' She wandered out on the landing and peered down into the hall. 'Crispin!'

'I found him in the village shop. The silly boy wasn't sure we'd want to see him but I told him that was rubbish.'

'Absolutely.' When she hurried down to join them it took all her self-control not to hug him.

'Rhonda passed on your letter when I popped in to see her the other day.' The ex-soldier kept his head down so she couldn't read his expression.

They'd spent hours debating what to do about Aled Jones' message before deciding to get in touch with Crispin's sister. They hoped she might talk him into sorting out his problems with the army once and for all. 'Aled sounded fond of you ... Cornflake.' A glimmer of amusement brightened his dark, hooded eyes when he glanced up. 'What he said made sense to us.'

'It's all right for him to talk.'

'We've had a good old chat walking back here,' Polly

jumped in. 'I told him it doesn't do any good to sweep problems under the rug. Me and Jack learned our lesson the hard way when we didn't talk about losing our Danny.'

Nessa was stunned. That tragic subject was still thorny ground. 'Are you staying, Crispin?'

'If you don't mind?' A mottled rash coloured his neck. 'Only until I sort myself out and I don't mean a couple of years this time around. Maybe a week at most?'

'Stay as long as you like. We've missed you. Did Polly tell you about our new enterprise?'

'Yeah. Amazing how much news she can cram into a ten-minute walk.' He struggled with the semblance of a smile. 'Your American's coming back soon – for good?'

No doubt he'd been prompted to ask because Nessa's evasive replies when Polly asked the same thing had about killed her friend. 'Don't worry, we've kept your camping spot free.' That abrupt turn in the conversation earned her knowing looks.

'Cheers. I'll get settled and I'll be over in the morning to see what needs doing.' Crispin nodded and disappeared out the door.

'Bit of a turn up for the books isn't it?' Polly said.

'I'm relieved. He's been on my mind a lot lately.'

'You mean there's room in that head of yours for other things than counting the hours until Romeo returns.' She made a grab for Nessa's left hand. 'Is he bringing back something sparkly for that empty finger?'

Lying didn't suit her so she resorted to silence.

'Thought so.' Polly oozed smugness.

'I'm going to pick some of those deep red

chrysanthemums for my bedroom.' Nessa tilted her chin and stalked out, followed by her friend's wicked laugh.

'The poor girl will have a fit if you turn up with us in tow,'

Ward grudgingly accepted his father was right. He'd thought it would be a wonderful surprise to bring his parents along when he returned to Cornwall next week but they'd thrown cold water on the idea.

'You know we'd love nothing better than to meet Nessa but you must ask first to make sure she wouldn't prefer us to wait a bit.' His mother's reasoning made sense.

'Okay I'll give her a call.' Although he'd missed Nessa dreadfully his folks had been great sounding boards for his new life plans. If they were disappointed that both of their children planned to live four thousand miles away for the foreseeable future they kept it to themselves. More than once their unselfish love forced him to bite back tears. He saw now with shocking clarity that the so-called love between him and Sophia had been nothing but an illusion.

Ward calculated the time difference and pulled out his phone. 'I'll talk to her now.'

'We'll leave you to it.' His mother shooed her husband towards the door. 'Good luck.'

Massive elephants stomped around his stomach which was crazy because he was so in tune with Nessa he could predict her reaction. She'd be happy with an undercurrent of nerves about whether or not his parents would like her.

'What a lovely surprise. I didn't expect to hear from you until later.'

Hearing her voice lifted his spirits and he instantly

poured out his question. 'Mom told me off for assuming it'd be okay.'

'That's thoughtful of her but of course I'd love to meet them. I'll be a bit anxious but that's normal. They must wonder what I'm like too.'

'They're lookin' forward to spending time with Ashley as well. They've been worried about her and it'll reassure them to see how she's doin'. But this doesn't mean I'll leave you alone in that lovely big bed any longer. Don't even think about arguing because I promise they won't think any less of you.' Her brief silence registered.

'I see your intuition still works long distance.' The flippant remark didn't fool him. 'I'm still working on my not-needing-to-please-everyone skills.'

'We'll do it together.'

They chatted some more and drifted into whispering hushed promises that made his blood heat.

'Sorry but I've got to go as someone's at the door. No rest for the wicked.'

'You're wicked all right and a mean woman to leave me hangin' that way.' His playful gripe made her laugh.

'It'll make you hurry back to Cornwall sooner. Love you lots.'

'Love you too. Witch,' Ward grumbled down the phone then realised he was talking to empty air. Time to break the good news to his parents. He'd call her back later and get his revenge.

Nessa fretted while she weeded the carrots. She'd never been faced with the meet-the-parents problem because the few brief romances she'd had along the way never reached that point and she'd known Jago Teague and his family forever. If she asked Lowena for advice she would be whisked off to the hairdresser and manicurist and turned into a polished, unnatural version of herself. Was she naïve to think those things didn't matter?

'Hi, Aunt Nessa.' Kit loped in through the garden. 'I looked for you down at the house but I don't know why I didn't think to check here first.'

'Is everything all right?'

'Yeah but I need some advice.' Her nephew turned pink. 'Girl stuff.'

Nessa stood up and dusted off her jeans. 'Let's sit on the bench. Your Granny Vivian likes to keep up with what's going on.' He gave her the look teenagers reserved for adults they thought were loopy. 'What's up?' He plopped down next to her. 'Is there a girl you like at college?'

'Yep. Her name's Lucy and we're on the same course. I asked her out and she said yes but I don't know where to take her or what to say or wear or anything.' Panic made his voice turn shrill. 'I can't ask Mum because she's busy and anyway she'd be embarrassing.' His blush deepened to a hot shade of crimson. 'She'd probably give me condoms and a lecture.' Kit planted his hands on his knees. 'Don't suggest Dad – he's worse than useless.'

He looked offended when Nessa grinned until she explained she wasn't laughing *at* him but the fact they were in a similar position. By the time she rattled off her own dilemma they were both in fits of laughter. They ended up deciding that a walk along the cliff path followed by coffee at a beach café would be the perfect low-key first date. 'Ask her about herself, her career plans, her family –

anything really to show you're genuinely interested in her and her opinions.' Nessa touched his hand. 'Remember she'll be nervous too.' She shook her head. 'I'm so stupid. I've answered my own questions talking to you. All we need to do is stay true to ourselves.'

'You're okay as you are. You don't fuss about stuff and you don't nag.' Kit kept his eyes on the ground and kicked at a stone.

Her throat tightened. Compliments from seventeen-year-old boys were rare and priceless. 'I made a carrot and rosemary cake earlier. It's a new recipe for my course and I need a taste tester. Care to volunteer?'

'Yeah if you make me.'

As they walked away she noticed the first leaves turning yellow on one of the old oaks. Autumn was starting to creep in but what a summer it'd been.

Chapter Twenty-Seven

'Are you comin' with us, Ash?' Ward set down his empty coffee mug. 'Lowena and Kit are down at the farm already. Mom and Dad should be almost ready if she's made up her mind what to wear.'

Yesterday their parents were exhausted after the long journey so he'd taken advantage and popped down to see Nessa. He didn't come home again until it was time for breakfast.

'Please. You'll help deflect the inquisition from Nessa.'

'Fine I'll come. Hopefully if they're busy checking her out it might stop them watching me for a few minutes.'

He sympathised with his sister's frustration but also understood where their parents were coming from.

'I bet the poor girl is shaking.' Ashley's wry smile returned. 'I'm never goin' through that rigmarole again. Bunny's parents never thought I was good enough for their precious son. I've no idea what he told them about our break-up and I don't care. They can spread all the stories they want about me being a useless, unfaithful wife. I'm shot of him and that's all I care about.'

Ward hated the thought of his beautiful, smart sister being alone for the rest of her life but maybe it was better than the alternative – who was he to say?

'We're ready, son. Let's go meet your lady love.' His father bustled in and yelled back over his shoulder. 'Come on, Fiona or young Nessa will think we're bad-mannered Americans and it'll be a mark against our boy.'

'I'm here, Todd. Stop fretting.' His mother breezed in.

'Ward is head over heels in love with her so she can't be that sort of woman.' She gave him a knowing look. 'He's got more sense these days.'

'Sure do, Mom. Do you want to walk or ride?' They were blessed with mild weather for late October and he wanted to show off the stunning views over the Polgarth Valley.

'Walk. I need some fresh air.' His mother rubbed at her lower back. 'I'm stiff as a board after all that travelling.'

They set off and he couldn't help thinking that none of them could've predicted this six months ago when he was still in Nashville and struggling to find a new path in life and Ashley was stuck in her dismal marriage. Their parents must rest easier these days.

'Here we are. Pear Tree Farm.' Ward led the way in through the gate and a flutter of nerves set up in the pit of his stomach. He'd texted to say they were on their way and on cue the farmhouse door opened. Nessa gave them a cheery wave as she stepped out to join them and vivid memories of the day they met sneaked in to reassure him. She'd been so kind when he made a fool of himself and he suspected in a tiny corner of his heart he'd fallen in love with her then.

In the bustle of introducing everyone Ward managed to whisper in her ear and stake his claim to a few minutes alone with her after lunch, in the pear orchard.

'We're eating in the dining room today because it would be a bit of a squash in the kitchen plus it will give you the chance to see Ward's handiwork. He painted the walls for me last month which was incredibly kind of him because he must've been sick to death of decorating after doing so much at Tregereth. What do you think of the house by the way?'

'It's awesome.' His mother's proud smile radiated through the room. 'My kids have done a great job ... not forgetting Lowena of course who's incredible. We're in the Bluebell Room.'

Nessa raised an eyebrow at him.

'While I was gone the ladies gave all our guest rooms names after flowers that grow in the grounds so I'm informed the others are Daffodil, Rhododendron, Hydrangea and Rose.'

'We're picking up the flower names in the soft furnishings and other décor.' Lowena's satisfied smile amused Ward. 'We chivvied George Yeatman and his plumber along to get the first of the en-suites installed so the only thing Mr and Mrs Spencer are missing out on is the floor looking as it should. That's on the schedule to be done by Christmas.'

And woe betide poor George if it isn't, he thought. He'd been amazed by how much they'd achieved in the three weeks he'd been gone but it was easier to understood when his poor builder stopped by this morning to give him an update looking distinctly thinner and fraught around the edges.

He draped an arm around Nessa's shoulder. 'C'mon let's eat, I'm starved.'

'Good to see him fillin' out again.' Todd's blunt declaration was embarrassing.

'Feel free to talk about me as though I'm not here.' His fake grumble made everyone laugh. 'What've you whipped up for lunch anyway?'

'You know what we're having because you put in the order.' Nessa grinned at his parents. 'He insisted you'd enjoy sampling a genuine Cornish pasty so I hope he's right. If you discover you don't like it I won't be offended. I've also got plenty of cold ham, a variety of local cheeses and salad.'

'Lead me to it,' his father said. 'The boy wouldn't let us try one at the train station. He said we had to eat the proper thing first.'

Ward found himself sat at one end of the gleaming mahogany table, a family heirloom passed down through the Vivian family for generations, with Nessa opposite. It struck him how awesome the room would look with a fresh Christmas tree filling the corner by the window and their families gathered around. If the picture came true maybe there would be a baby in Nessa's arms with her dark hair and sparkling jade eyes. He jolted back to the here and now when his father stood up and raised his glass.

'I want to propose a toast to the cook.' He patted his stomach. 'You've converted me to pasties and I look forward to eatin' plenty more.'

'You'll be welcome anytime.'

Ward lifted his beer glass and nodded at Nessa, swapping silent promises with her.

'Here you go.' Nessa plucked the ripest pear off the tree and offered it to him. 'That's your reward for keeping your promise.' She picked another for herself and watched him bite into the juicy fruit before she started on her own.

'They're amazing. The best I've ever tasted. So sweet.' His gaze bored into her. 'Like you.'

201

Nessa glanced towards the bench. 'Should we?'

'Yeah, I reckon so.'

They carried on munching and tossed the cores onto the compost heap.

'The gravel's too rough to kneel on so I recommend you stay sitting.' She hadn't missed him patting his right trouser pocket every few minutes.

'Aren't you goin' to act surprised?'

'Why?'

Ward shrugged. 'I don't know. Tradition?'

She grabbed his face and planted a long, lingering kiss on his mouth. 'We're not that way or we wouldn't be crazy enough to get engaged this fast.'

'Getting engaged are we?' The fake surprise he injected into his voice made her laugh. 'Is that what this is for?' A small red velvet box appeared in his hand. 'I wondered what it was doin' in my pocket all this time but now I know it was waiting for you.' He popped open the lid. 'Will this persuade you to marry me? The topaz reminded me of your pears.'

'It's gorgeous. I do believe it might do the trick.' Nessa held out her hand then noticed his were shaking and helped him slip the ring in place. She peered at the stunning golden stone surrounded by sparkling diamonds. 'It's working quite well.'

'Only quite? If you're not totally convinced I do have something else planned to help us celebrate. I'm not a complete loser.'

She turned around to see who he was beckoning over her shoulder and gasped in shock. Somehow their families had sneaked up to join them and when she spotted Polly,

202

Jack and Crispin hovering in the background, tears pricked at her eyes. 'Oh I love you so much.' Nessa flung her arms around him.

Ward's father walked toward them carrying a bottle of champagne in each hand followed by Lowena with a tray of glasses. It didn't take long to pop the corks and make sure everyone had a drink.

'Polly and your mum have hit it off but Ashley's looking a bit left out.' His sister was hanging back by the wall sipping her champagne. 'I'll go and talk to her. Why don't you have a word with Crispin? I still can't believe they managed to drag him here.'

'I can. He thinks the world of you. I'll go over and thank him for coming so that gives him an out if he wants to escape.'

She popped a kiss on his cheek. 'You're sweet even if you sometimes try to cover it up. See you back here in a few minutes.' Nessa made her way to Ashley. 'This was a lovely surprise. Not the proposal bit because I expected that but all of you joining in.'

'My brother's the best.' Ashley sounded wistful. 'I'm super happy you found each other.'

'Me too.'

'Sweetheart, this guy wants a quick word.' Ward tugged Crispin forward. 'Sorry, Ash I forgot you two don't know each other.' He rattled off quick introductions and Nessa picked up on Ashley and Crispin's mutual awkwardness. Neither wanted to be the first to speak or shake hands.

'Thanks for coming, Crispin. I really appreciate it.' Out of the corner of her eye she noticed Ashley studying him.

'No problem.'

On a normal day his eyes were barely visible under his mop of thick, shaggy hair but today she couldn't miss their startling, dark blue depths. His hair was buzzed off to a dark shadow and the thick full beard was history too. Nessa blushed when he caught her staring.

'I'm leaving first thing tomorrow to turn myself in. That accounts for this.' He stroked his bare chin. 'You were right. It's the only way.' Crispin heaved a deep sigh.

'You've always got a home back here when you're done with the army.'

'I'm not sure when that'll be but thanks. For everything.'

She wouldn't force a goodbye on him.

'I've had a word with Polly and Jack.'

That was a step forward. 'Take care of yourself.' Nessa tried to smile while fighting back tears.

Crispin nodded and scuttled away, avoiding everyone on his way out.

'That's the guy you told me about?' A tinge of heat coloured Ashley's cheeks. 'He's not what I expected.'

'How so?' Ward asked.

'The haircut I guess.'

Nessa guessed it might've been on the tip of his sister's tongue to say Crispin was an extremely good-looking man but kept that speculation to herself.

'I ought to be going,' Ashley said. 'Lowena's got me on freezer stocking duty today. I'm goin' to learn how to make scones and sausage rolls. No regular old triangular American scones either because that's apparently an abomination.' Her eyes twinkled. 'I suspect it could be a trial run for your wedding reception. I hope we don't have too long to wait.'

'I don't know.' Her cheeks blazed. 'We haven't discussed it yet.'

Ward's arm tightened around her shoulders. 'I sure don't want to hang around if that's okay with the future Mrs Spencer?'

She met his searing gaze and if there'd been a vicar on hand she would've married him on the spot. 'Isn't it funny how much we agree on these days?'

'I'd call it awesome.' His smile was brighter than the sun. 'We've got a lot to thank old Bill Tremayne for.'

'We certainly do.'

Thank You

As always, I appreciate the Choc Lit Tasting Panel who fell in love with Nessa and Ward's story and who are ready to head off to Cornwall to stay at Pear Tree Farm! I also want to say a big thank you to everyone who chooses to read my books. If you enjoyed Nessa and Ward's story and have a minute to leave a review on the site where you bought the book or Goodreads, that would be amazing.

Angela

x

About the Author

Angela was born in St. Stephen, Cornwall, England.
After completing her A-Levels she worked as a Naval
Secretary. She met her husband, a US Naval Flight Officer
while being based at a small NATO Headquarters on
the Jutland Peninsula in Denmark. They lived together
in Denmark, Sicily, California, southern Maryland
and London before settling in Franklin, Tennessee.

Angela took a creative writing course in 2000 and loved
it so much that she has barely put her pen down since.
She has had short stories and novels published in the US.
Her debut novel, *Sugar & Spice*, won Choc Lit's Search
for an American Star competition and is her UK debut.

Follow Angela:
Twitter: www.twitter.com/AngelaBritnell
Facebook: www.facebook.com/angelabritnell

More Choc Lit

From Angela Britnell

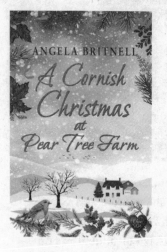

A Cornish Christmas at Pear Tree Farm

Sequel to *A Cornish Summer at Pear Tree Farm*

Pairing up at Pear Tree Farm in time for Christmas …

Pear Tree Farm in Cornwall, owned by the kind-hearted Nessa Vivian, is known for taking in lost souls, and ex-soldier Crispin Davies is certainly one of those. But the once sleepy caravan park is now a thriving business, and far from the peace and quiet Crispin was craving, he soon finds himself roped into helping out with a short-notice Christmas festival, organised by Nessa's force-of-nature sister, Lowena.

But despite Crispin's initial reluctance, his involvement in the festival serves to throw him together with Ashley Spencer, an American woman and fellow lost soul, who works at the nearby Tregereth House. Could Lowena's ambitious scheme result in a more hopeful Christmas and New Year for them both – with a few surprises along the way?

Visit www.choc-lit.com for details.

Spring on Rendezvous Lane

Can even the most seasoned traveller find a home on Rendezvous Lane?

'Community spirit' is not a phrase in travel junkie Taran Rossi's vocabulary. As a former 'third culture kid' and now spicy street food connoisseur and social media influencer, he's never really stayed in one place long enough to feel part of a community. And that's just the way he likes it. But a springtime stint house sitting for his grandmother on Rendezvous Lane in East Nashville could lead to a long overdue wake-up call. With the help of single mum Sandy Warner and her young son Chip, can Taran come to understand that sometimes it's not about the place – it's about the people?

One Summer in Little Penhaven

Book 1 in the Little Penhaven series

Could one summer change your life?

When high-flying American lawyer Samantha Muir finds out she's lost her partnership whilst on an assignment in London, she has a dramatic reaction. Rather than returning home, she resigns, leaves her business suits behind and jumps on the first train to Cornwall at the encouragement of a friendly stranger.

The village of Little Penhaven, where Samantha eventually ends up, is a world away from her life in Knoxville, Tennessee – and local farmer Cadan Day is certainly a world away from any man she has met before. But could the Cornish village and Cadan play a part in Samantha's summer of self-discovery?

Visit www.choc-lit.com for details.

Christmas in Little Penhaven

Book 2 in the Little Penhaven series

Have yourself a little Cornish Christmas …
Wannabe author Jane Solomon is expecting an uneventful Christmas in her Cornish village of Little Penhaven.

But then super fit American gym owner Hal Muir comes to town, and suddenly the holiday season looks set to be far more interesting. Hal is keen on embracing every British tradition on offer, from mince pies to Christmas pub quizzes – and perhaps some festive romance too …

A Summer to Remember in Herring Bay

Essy Havers is good at finding things. Her company specialises in helping clients track down anything, from missing china pieces to rare vintage clothing. But now Essy has something more important to find: herself.

Essy has always been curious about her mother's secret past and her Cornish roots. So, when the opportunity arises, she hops on a plane in Tennessee and ends up in Herring Bay in Cornwall; the village where her mother grew up.

But once there, she's mystified by the reactions of the villagers when they realise who she is. Was Essy's decision to visit Cornwall a mistake, or will it lead to a summer she'll never forget?

Visit www.choc-lit.com for details.

Christmas at Moonshine Hollow

Mistletoe and moonshine: a Christmas match made in heaven?

Moonshine Hollow's famous 'Lightning Flash' might be an acquired taste, although the same could be said for moonshine distillery owner Cole Landon, what with his workaholic habits and 'Scrooge' tendencies when it comes to all things Christmassy.

But when Jenna Pendean from Cornwall pays a visit to Cole's family-run distillery in Tennessee during the holiday season, will Cole's cynicism about the existence of Christmas miracles be put to the test?

Christmas at Black Cherry Retreat

What if you had nowhere to call home for Christmas?

When Fee Winter books a winter break at the remote Black Cherry Retreat in the small town of Pine Ridge, Tennessee, it's with the idea that the peace and quiet will help her recuperate from her hectic life as a photographer.

But what she didn't bank on was meeting Tom Chambers and his huge, interfering yet lovable family. With them, could Fee finally experience the warmth and support that's been missing from her own life – and maybe even find a place to call home in time for Christmas?

Visit www.choc-lit.com for details.

Sugar and Spice

The Way to a Hero's Heart …

Fiery, workaholic Lily Redman wants more than anything to make a success of her new American TV show, Celebrity Chef Swap – without the help of her cheating ex-fiancé and producer, Patrick O'Brien.

Kenan Rowse is definitely not looking for love. Back from a military stint in Afghanistan and recovering from a messy divorce, the last thing he needs is another complication. So when he lands a temporary job as Luscious Lily's driver, he's none too pleased to find that they can't keep their hands off each other!

But trudging around Cornish farms, knee deep in mud, and meetings with egotistical chefs was never going to be the perfect recipe for love – was it? And Lily could never fall for a man so disinterested in food – could she?

What Happens in Nashville

'What happens in Nashville, stays in Nashville!'

Claire Buchan is hardly over the moon about the prospect of her sister's hen party in Nashville. Certainly not straight-laced Claire's idea of a good time, what with her lawyer job and sensible boyfriend, Philip.

But then she doesn't bank on meeting Rafe Castello. As he and Claire get to know each other, she realises there is far more to him than meets the eye.

Can Claire keep to the holiday mantra of 'what happens in Nashville, stays in Nashville' or will she find that some things are far too difficult to simply leave behind?

Visit www.choc-lit.com for details.

Celtic Love Knot

Can two tangled lives make a love knot?
Lanyon Tremayne is the outcast of his small Cornish village of St. Agnes. Nobody knows the painful secret he hides.

Olivia Harding has learnt a thing or two about ogres. She's a professor from Tennessee, specialising in Celtic mythology and has come to St. Agnes to research the legend of a Cornish giant – and to lay to rest a couple of painful secrets of her own.

But when Olivia meets the ruggedly handsome Lanyon, her trip to Cornwall looks set to become even more interesting. Will she get through to the man beneath the bad-tempered façade, or is Lanyon fated to be the 'ogre' of St. Agnes forever?

The Wedding Reject Table

Once on the reject table, always on the reject table?
When Maggie Taylor, a cake decorator, and Chad Robertson, a lawyer from Nashville Tennessee, meet at a wedding in Cornwall it's not under the best circumstances.

They have both been assigned to 'the reject table', alongside a toxic collection of grumpy great aunts, bitter divorcees and stuffy organists.

Maggie has grown used to being the reject, although when Chad helps her out of a wedding cake disaster she begins to wonder whether the future could hold more for her.

But will Chad be strong enough to deal with the other problems in Maggie's life? Because a ruined cake isn't the only issue she has – not by a long shot.

Visit www.choc-lit.com for details.

Here Comes the Best Man

Being the best man is a lot to live up to …
When troubled army veteran and musician Josh Robertson returns home to Nashville to be the best man at his younger brother Chad's wedding he's just sure that he's going to mess it all up somehow.

But when it becomes clear that the wedding might not be going to plan, it's up to Josh and fellow guest Louise Giles to make sure that Chad and his wife-to-be Maggie get their perfect day.

Can Josh be the best man his brother needs? And is there somebody else who is beginning to realise that Josh could be her 'best man' too?

Love Me for a Reason

Love doesn't always have to make sense …
When Daisy Penvean meets Nathaniel Dalton whilst visiting a friend in Nashville, it seems there are a million and one reasons for them not to be together. Nathaniel's job as a mergers and acquisitions manager means sharp suits and immaculate hair, whereas Daisy's work as a children's book illustrator lends itself to a more carefree, laid-back style. And, as Daisy lives in England, there's also the small matter of the Atlantic Ocean between them.

But when Nathaniel's job takes him to London, he and Daisy meet again under very different circumstances. Because Daisy works for the publisher involved in the deal, and if Nathaniel does his job, it could mean she loses hers …

Visit www.choc-lit.com for details.

You're The One That I Want

What if you didn't want to fake it any more?

When Sarah, a teacher from Cornwall, and Matt, a businessman from Nashville, meet on a European coach tour, they soon find themselves in a relationship …

Except it's a fake relationship. Because Matt is too busy for romance, and Sarah is only trying to make her cheating ex-husband jealous … isn't she?

As Matt and Sarah complete their tour of Europe, they do all the things real couples are supposed to do.

But as their holiday comes to an end, Sarah and Matt realise that they're not happy with their pretend relationship. They want the real thing.

New Year New Guy

Out with the old life, in with the new …

When Laura's bride-to-be sister, Polly, organises a surprise reunion for her fiancé and his long lost American friend, Laura grudgingly agrees to help keep the secret. And when the plain-spoken, larger-than-life Hunter McQueen steps off the bus in her rainy Devon town and only just squeezes into her tiny car, it confirms that Laura has made a big mistake in going along with her sister's crazy plan.

But could the tall, handsome man with the Nashville drawl be just what reserved Laura Williams needs to shake up her life and start something new?

Visit www.choc-lit.com for details.

Introducing Choc Lit

We're an independent publisher creating
a delicious selection of fiction.
Where heroes are like chocolate – irresistible!
Quality stories with a romance at the heart.

See our selection here:
www.choc-lit.com

We'd love to hear how you enjoyed *A Cornish Summer at Pear Tree Farm*. Please visit **www.choc-lit.com** and give your feedback or leave a review where you purchased this novel.

Choc Lit novels are selected by genuine readers like yourself. We only publish stories our Choc Lit Tasting Panel want to see in print. Our reviews and awards speak for themselves.

Could you be a Star Selector and join our Tasting Panel?
Would you like to play a role in choosing which novels
we decide to publish? Do you enjoy reading women's
fiction? Then you could be perfect for our Tasting Panel.

Visit here for more details…
www.choc-lit.com/join-the-choc-lit-tasting-panel

Keep in touch:
Sign up for our monthly newsletter Spread for all the latest
news and offers: www.spread.choc-lit.com.
Follow us on Twitter: @ChocLituk,
Facebook: Choc Lit and Instagram: @ChocLituk.

Where heroes are like chocolate – irresistible!